IVY'S SAVAGE LUST

TOO HOT TO HANDLE

OTTAVIANO CRIME FAMILY

NOA CAMHI
LASHE LACROIX

JOIN OUR NEWSLETTER

Be the first to hear about new releases, exclusive offers, and giveaways. Click the link below to get a free copy of **Callum's Vow.**

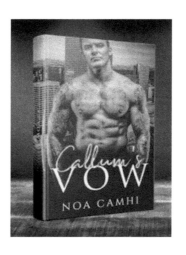

Sign up here. **https://noacamhi.gr8.com/**

Join Lashe Lacroix newsletter to receive a free copy of **Betrayed by Alcino.**

Sign up here. **https://dl.bookfunnel.com/xvx6dx3pqw**

ABOUT TOO HOT TO HANDLE

"Romance Bunnies is delighted to announce the
Too Hot to Handle Series.

Lay back on the beach, imagine you are in the exclusive
resort of Pāʻina Exclusive Resort on the Pāʻina Island in
Hawaii, grab your cocktail and lose yourself in the 9
novellas that are full of steamy, sexy romance.

Is the resort too hot, too steamy, too much for you to
handle? Dive right in and find out.

What happens in the Pāʻina Exclusive Resort doesn't
always stay there! Read all 9 stories in the Too Hot to
Handle series to find out if you can handle the heat!"

I had a one-night stand with a stranger...
He's a mafia Don...
He's my ex's father...
My addiction...

Ivy Johnson

My knight in shining armor turned out to be my ex's
father. One night of savage passion led me to my
addiction: Leonardo.

Except in the next morning, he was gone.

Back from vacation, I'm hit with some unexpected,
unsettling news. The recent stress wasn't the reason my
regular period was now six weeks late.

I'm called into my boss's office for a meeting. Instead of
seeing my perverted boss, it was Leonardo, holding a
pregnancy test in his hand.

Leonardo Ottaviano

Her light is a balm to my tattered soul. Dragging her into a mafia war wasn't what I had in mind when I met her.

When my enemies lock their sights on her, I have to make a choice: my revenge or her.

Just when I think things can't get worse, I find out Ivy has secrets of her own.

She belongs to me.

CHAPTER 1

IVY JOHNSON

MANHATTAN, NEW YORK

The barista snatched the latte off the counter and thrust it at me. Caramel, whipped cream, and coffee spilled. I looked down to see my new cream, silk, designer blouse ruined. My mouth opened as I tried to process the catastrophe at the same time my lace bra underneath started leaking.

Not today, Satan.

I quickly grabbed several napkins and attempted to stop the liquid from doing further damage. I knew it was already too late.

I can't believe this.

"I'm sorry. Today's crowd is busier than our normal Monday crowd. I thought the top was on it. Don't worry about paying for the drink it's on the house."

This top was the first expensive designer blouse I

had. It cost me three full paychecks just to buy it. Now the top was ruined. A year of free coffee couldn't replace what I spent for the top.

"Forget it. I don't want the drink anymore." After tossing the napkins in the trashcan, I rushed out of the coffee shop.

A fleeting glance at my watch confirmed that I had less than eight minutes to buy a blouse next door and get into the office. The door slammed behind me as I barged inside the boutique. Normally, I would agonize over my outfit and how it accentuated my thick curves but not today. Today was the day we would meet at the office before embarking on our company sponsored vacation. I snatched the first extra-large blouse off the hanger and ran to the cashier.

After placing the top on the counter, I took out my credit card. "Don't worry about a bag. I'm going to wear it."

She nodded. "I don't blame you. Your shirt looks like it got more coffee than you did."

After she handed me my receipt, I sprinted out of the shop.

It was another fifteen minutes before I had my luggage, purse, and badge in my hand. I raced across the parking lot sprinting in my stilettos.

Paul, our security guard, opened the door. "Don't worry about badging through. I know you're late. I'll manually clock in for you. You'd better hurry, most of your coworkers came thirty minutes early today."

"Paul, you're a lifesaver. Thanks. Today has been hectic."

I ran through the sensors and skidded to a halt in front of the elevators, as they opened. Ignoring the evil stares from the people inside, mentally I checked off everything I was supposed to take with me for the trip. By the time the elevator doors opened, I had calmed down. I exhaled, as I heard someone clear their throat. "Ivy, you're over twenty-seven minutes late. You are up for a promotion. This won't look good, and it might have compromised your opportunity to move up in the company," said John.

I have been working here for over nine years. Cut me some slack instead of dangling the elusive promotion that never comes in my face.

"I'm sorry John. My tire was going flat and I had to keep stopping to put air in it. I called roadside assistance but they told me it would take them three hours to get someone to me."

His eyes dropped to my blouse. "Lucky for you, I advised management that I had allowed you to come in a little later to handle some personal matters."

John Waters was my manager. He was also the biggest cock hound in the office. The only reason I hadn't been promoted before now was because I hadn't slept with him. All the women who worked here, had caved, and slept with him.

I stood up. "I appreciate it."

The door opened behind him, and Olivia walked in with her matching Versace bags. She looked amazing in a red silk wrap around dress that accentuated all her curves.

"Ivy are you ready? Is that all the luggage you're taking?

"Yes."

Matthew is waiting to help us with our luggage."

"Great. We shouldn't keep him waiting." Dragging my stuff behind me, I made my way to her.

John frowned. "I'll leave you to get yourself ready for the trip. I'll be flying out to the island later in the week, we can talk more then."

No. You can just leave me alone.

I watched him leave my office.

As soon as the door closed, I sighed. "Girl, you are a lifesaver. He was about to get on my nerves. Lately, he has been trying to spend time with me alone. I'm not for it. His actions are making me uncomfortable."

Today is not starting well. I hope Hawaii is as beautiful and peaceful as they say.

"I was worried that you changed your mind. I thought you had chickened out on me and stayed home to cry over your breakup."

You know me well. The thought crossed my mind several times.

"You were right. I haven't been to Hawaii and everything is better with clear blue water and pineapples. My personal life is in shambles but it doesn't have to ruin my vacation."

Olivia opened the door. "Just think, later today we will be in paradise. I'm nervous about finally meeting my boss in person. He already comes across as a type a, workaholic, smartass. Putting a face to a name is ridiculous at this point."

We arrived at La Guardia twenty minutes later despite not being far from the airport. The traffic here in the city was always horrendous.

As soon as she parked, I jumped out. "We need to hurry so that we can get through security and find the gate."

"I know but traffic was worse than usual. Do you have your identification and ticket?" asked Olivia.

After I pulled our luggage out of the trunk, I patted myself down. Once I heard the crumpling of my paper tickets, I sighed. "Yes. My tickets are in my front pocket. My driver's license is still in my purse, but it is easy to get to once we reach the security checkpoint."

I rolled her bags over to her. "You packed like you intend to move to Hawaii. You know you're going to want to shop and you won't have any room in your stuffed luggage."

She grabbed her bags. "I'll cross that bridge after we get there. If I need too, I will ship one of these bags to my house and buy more luggage to bring back my new stuff."

Chuckling, I followed her across the garage through the second parking to the elevator. The doors opened and we slid inside. I was relieved when the doors closed. There wasn't much room in the elevator because our bags took up all the space.

As soon as the doors opened, we ran down the ramp and went inside the airport double doors. We stepped on the escalator and headed down to the lower-level security gate.

When we reached the lower level, we stepped off and walked toward the gate. Olivia was ahead of me, and I increased my speed to keep up.

A man wearing a dark wide brimmed baseball cap bumped into me and ran away.

"What the heck?" I bit my lip to keep from cursing as I picked up my luggage.

Olivia frowned and waved to me as she stood behind the security agent. "Come on hurry up."

I skidded to a halt behind an elderly man walking on a cane.

"I need your ticket mam," said the guard.

My hand slid in my pocket, and I frowned. After releasing my luggage, I checked my other pocket. "My tickets are gone."

Olivia's eyes widened. "That guy that bumped you must have stolen your tickets."

"If you don't have a ticket, I'm afraid you're going to have to step out of the line," said the guard.

"There's no way that I can buy a roundtrip ticket to Hawaii at the last minute." I closed my eyes, fighting tears of frustration.

"Olivia, go on without me."

This was the last straw. I wiped the tears from my eyes, grabbed my luggage and stepped out of the line. Normally it would mortify me to be the center of attention, but now I didn't care. Someone had stolen my tickets.

How did I not see this coming? What made me an easy mark over everyone else in the airport?

I was getting ready to miss the plane. There was absolutely no way that I could afford a last-minute ticket. I was just barely surviving on ramen noodles, water, and beans. The designer blouse purchased had been with a part of my one-time performance bonus, which had been ruined. The company salary was ok but with my student loan, and living expenses in New York, I was living from paycheck to paycheck. My savings were a meager twelve hundred dollars, which wouldn't keep me off the street if I lost my job. Going to Hawaii would have been nice but I wish I had followed my first mind and stayed at home.

I had just broken up with my boyfriend Antonio after catching him screwing my friend. Now I've been robbed. I'm not sure how much more I can take.

With my head down, I strolled toward the escalators. I stopped when I remembered Olivia had driven us here. I would need to take an Uber back to the office to get my car.

Everyone is going to ask why I wasn't in Hawaii. I'd tell them that something came up and I had to go home.

Suddenly, Olivia grabbed my arm and swung me around. "Oh no you don't. Ivy, you're not leaving me in Hawaii by myself. We're going over there to the ticket counter and get you a last-minute ticket. Let's go."

She looked fierce. Within seconds she had snatched my luggage and rolled all the luggage to the ticket counter. There was a cute guy standing there waiting for the gate agent. He offered Olivia his place in line.

That would never happen to me.

Olivia was dropped dead gorgeous. The ideal beauty to most men wasn't a curvy, brown skinned woman with curly hair. Society pushed the standard beauty as thin with an athletic body type. My breasts and my thick thighs weighed more than her total body weight. It was the reason Antonio was cheating on me, with Sara the hundred- and twenty-pound aerobics instructor.

How could I have been stupid enough to believe he really liked me?

When Antonio had spoken of marriage and seeing us having a family with two kids, I believed him because he seemed genuine. Now, I realize it was all talk. I should have seen through the lies because it's been three years and he still hadn't given me an engagement ring.

I bit my lip harder as I felt the tears dampening my eyelashes. The last thing I needed was to fall apart standing in the middle of the airport. There would be time to weep in the back of the Uber car on the way back to the office.

After I was certain my tears were gone, I walked up behind Olivia.

"What do you mean it's going to be over forty-five hundred dollars for a ticket? My friend just had her ticket stolen. There must be something you can do?"

"I'm sorry Ms. Cruz. That is the last ticket on the same flight. To be honest if you don't book it soon, it won't be an option either," she said.

Olivia cursed. "Is there a way I could exchange my ticket from first class to coach and pay the difference in cost to her a ticket? Can I use my miles?"

"I'm afraid not. If it had been your ticket stolen then you could use your miles but your miles are not transferable. I don't have a seat in coach to offer you if you give up your seat. The plane has already arrived and should be boarding in the next ten minutes."

I grabbed her shoulder. "Just go board the plane. Have an amazing trip and call me. Keep a detailed itinerary so that the next time we can go as a girl's trip. At that time, I'll make sure I'm not robbed."

The only positive aspect in this situation was that at least my driver's license was still safely tucked in my purse. There was a line forming now and it didn't make sense to make others miss their flights because I had to miss mine.

"It doesn't make sense. Your ticket was stolen and used yet you're still here. This airport and airline should have more security than that. She can clearly see by your identification that you aren't on the plane," snapped Olivia.

Olivia tossed her hair over her shoulder. She took out her black card. "I have two thousand dollars of it. You need twenty-five hundred."

My mouth suddenly opened. Olivia spent money like she drank water. It was rare for her to offer to pay for anything. She was always spending money and I was humbled that she offered anything at all.

I shook my head. "I only have twelve hundred in my savings. It's not enough. We work at the same place but my salary is not as much as yours. "Let's not make a scene. Call me when you get there."

"There must be some other way. I'm not flying to Hawaii without you. I'm not dealing with this alone."

Massaging my temples, I prayed for patience. "Olivia only you would think that meeting your boss for the first time is an ordeal. It's in Hawaii. It's two seconds. Smile. Say "I'm Olivia, it's nice to meet you." Think about the pineapple drinks you're going to drink later." Without waiting for her excuse, I grabbed my luggage and headed for the escalators.

"Wait. Oh shit," said Olivia.

Turning around, I saw that she had run into a handsome guy. When she attempted to excuse herself, he didn't let her elbow go. Normally, I would have said something but he was drop dead gorgeous, and the epitome of tall, dark, and handsome. He had gorgeous glowing skin, crisp glossy hair that framed his face, and stunning blue eyes. My eyes traveled lower and I found it hard to swallow. His body looked amazing. Most men wore suits but his suit was wearing him. I don't know what kind of fabric it was but I was instantly jealous of it. There wasn't a part of him that I didn't want to feel, taste or caress.

He caught me staring. His lips curved.

I looked down quickly. Heat instantly rushed up my face and neck. Whenever I was embarrassed, I blushed profusely. I was certain my face was as red as a fire hydrant. It was obvious I had been eye fucking him. If I were a bold woman I would go over there and match my words with my heated looks. However, I was an extremely shy introvert who lacked confidence.

I'm a wallflower.

His whole demeanor commanded my attention and as soon as he gave it to me, I was instantly catapulted back to reality. I was a curvy girl, the bridesmaid not the bride, the girl next door, and immediately friend zoned.

My gifts and talents are always appreciated and coveted but unfortunately, they come in this package. A girl like me doesn't attract a handsome man like him.

The fact that he was wealthy and I was a struggling investment analyst only highlighted another reason to ignore the powerful attraction I had for him. The only thing I would experience would be shame, resentment, and heart break.

I cleared my throat. "Olivia, you're going to miss your flight."

She frowned at me and looked down at the hand that gripped her elbow. "This is America, and my blouse is Balenciaga. Release me now before I scream for security."

The man seemed to have gripped her elbow tighter.

"Marsha, give the woman the first-class seat," he said.

"Yes sir, right away."

Usually, I would've flagged down security or at least shouted for help. Instead, I was staring at the man like crazy with my freaking thong soaked. There were parts of me that were tingling that had never come to life before. This man's presence was like gluing a wand vibrator to my clit. Every part of me was soaked, trembling, and needing his attention. We locked eyes again, but this time, his lips curved as he took his time to take me all in. Everywhere his eyes roamed over me was like a heated drop of wax on my skin.

"Ms. Johnson, here is your ticket. They have started boarding the plane and the pilot is scheduled to leave on time. You two will need to hurry through security if you want to catch this flight."

She cleared her throat. "Ms. Johnson, here's your ticket."

"Ivy, snap out of it," said Olivia.

The sharpness in her voice snapped me out of the trance. I got the ticket. "Thank you."

Smiling at Olivia, I turned and rolled my luggage in the direction of the handsome man who paid for my plane ticket. This was my chance to thank him and hopefully, give him my phone number. I wasn't certain I wouldn't chicken out on giving him my number but I was going to thank him. I owed him that much.

I took several steps toward him before I ran into a solid wall of muscle. "Excuse me. I'd like to talk to the man standing behind you."

"As you can see, he's on the phone. I'll relay your thanks."

My eyes narrowed.

Who did this asshat think he was. His parents obviously hadn't taught him manners,

I opened my mouth to say just that until I noticed the not so hidden print of a gun behind his double-breasted jacket.

On second thought, I decided against it.

"Thanks." I turned and rushed behind Olivia toward the security checkpoint.

CHAPTER 2

LEONARDO OTTAVIANO

MANHATTAN, NEW YORK

*M*y time was up. I knew that this day was coming and I couldn't delay it any longer. It was time for me to meet Luca Cattaneo. The Cattaneos were the most powerful mafia family in New York. I didn't need to have any problems right now. My flight was scheduled to depart in less than two hours. Although I owned the airline, and every pilot knew better than to leave me, it didn't mean that I would be late. Time was a valuable commodity that you could never get back, which was why I never wasted it. The few foolish individuals that wasted my time, hadn't lived long enough to waste anyone else's. This meeting meant that Luca was prepared to make a move on me if I didn't leave New York.

I was currently fighting with the Borisov family. The Russian Bratva held grudges until death and they were sneaky, and unethical. They used tactics like killing wives and children to torture their enemies. I should know. Ioakim Borisov, the Pakhan, killed my wife, Giselle, with a car bomb meant for me. Every day since then, I've regretted his failure. My wife paid for my mistakes in blood. I was unable to confirm who put the bomb underneath my car, therefore I continued to fail her.

When will her soul be able to rest?

Luca had an alliance with the Vinogradov Bratva, Irish, and even some other cartel connections if my information was correct. If Viktor Vinogradov used his Russian connections to take me out, my family was in trouble. Luca had been smart. He formed an alliance with the Russians and Irish while maintaining a strong connection with the Italians. They were a superpower and damn near undefeatable. They would have to be destroyed from within. The Ottaviano family wasn't going anywhere.

I don't want to destroy them. I want to join them. What do they want more than my leaving New York?

Cosimo Panicucci walked inside the front door, with two dozen of my men in tow. It was time to leave. I finished my shot of brandy. "As I said, this is just a meeting. I'm not looking to start a war today. I have a feeling a war is not what Luca wants, but he'll not shy away from it either. Let me do all the talking. No one spills a drop of blood unless I give the go ahead."

Cosimo nodded. "Of course, boss. I sent two dozen men ahead of us to stake out the place and wait. They were supposed to check in an hour ago."

That is what I'm talking about!

Shaking my head, I counted to five before speaking again. I was dangerously close to killing Cosimo for his epic mistake. "I didn't tell you to do that. Your actions can be seen as an act of war. From this point on, no one does anything without my consent regardless of how trivial it seems."

He flushed and lowered his head. "Sorry boss. I always have our meetings staked out. I didn't think this one was any different. I'm sorry."

"It's done now. I don't intend to have this talk again with any of you. If this happens again, it will be a fatal mistake." After staring each of them down, I signaled for them to leave the house. It was time to go. I was ready to get this meeting over. I needed to plan my next move.

"Do you want me to call the men one more time before we leave?" asked Cosimo.

"No, they're already dead."

Twenty minutes later, we arrived at Momma Mia Pizza Parlor. I could feel eyes on me as soon as I stepped out of the car. No doubt it was from the barrel of a scope. This was an excellent location for a sniper ambush. I had no doubt the snipers had their sights on me.

I waved to them and entered the restaurant.

Every man was afraid of something, and I was no different. Too bad that something wasn't death. Ignoring his people posing as innocent bystanders, I made my way to the back table where Luca sat.

Pulling out a chair, I sat down. "Mr. Cattaneo, it's nice to finally meet you."

His eyes narrowed. "Cut the crap Leonardo. You've set up shop here and you've ignored all my warnings to leave. This territory is already occupied."

I leaned back. "I have ignored your suggestions."

Luca growled. "They weren't suggestions."

Out of the corner of my eye, I saw my men tense. Luca's tone was loud and disrespectful. I could tell he was ready to stop talking and start shooting. I had no doubt that if that happened the chances of my men and I leaving alive was slim to none. He had the advantage and his snipers had their lock on us. Their infrared dots hadn't appeared but I could feel them just the same. If I wanted us to leave here alive without bloodshed, I would need to be candid and truthful regardless of how Luca felt.

"I'm not going to leave New York. Your business has nothing to do with mine. Your family is powerful but so is the Ottaviano family. I'm not your enemy. The businesses we control would not step on your feet and run outside of your territory. You're upset because I've tilted the financial balance toward the

Italians which makes the Russians, and the Irish uneasy."

He leaned forward. "You don't get to tilt the financial balance in our territory. I'm sure you've come here today because you know that going to war with us is futile."

I snorted. "I don't know any such thing. If it's a war you want it's a war you can get. If you think your alliance scares me, it doesn't. I know all about your connections but you have no earthly idea about mine. Your assumption that we can't win a war with your alliance is a miscalculation. The Ottaviano family is here to stay. Instead of viewing us as an enemy, it would behoove you to view us as a potential ally. I'll let you think about it so that the next time we meet it can be a fruitful one."

I stood up. After gesturing to my men, I strolled out of the door. I was certain he wanted to put a bullet in the back of my head. I was also confident that he wouldn't. He wasn't the type of man to shoot someone like a coward. Luca wasn't a coward and he liked to get his hands dirty. Funny thing about it was that he and I had a lot in common. I'd hoped he would figure it out.

Within minutes, I was back in the Rolls Royce. It hadn't taken Cosimo long to double check the car before we went inside. Despite car bombs being easily detectable and cowardly, there were still mafia members who used them. In life there were no rules and the old rules that used to govern how Dons acted had been thrown out the window as each new generation took over the family business.

By the time we switched cars, I had retrieved my luggage. We were on time when we arrived at the airport. In addition, two of my men were already checking the plane. I always had several rotating men who secretly traveled with me on all flights, as well as two additional pilots aboard. The third part of my security plan was checking the passenger list and running it against my database to make sure there were no assassins on board.

I entered the airport through the secret door. After a swift retinal scan, I entered the administrative offices of HO Airlines. Nathaniel Esposito greeted me.

"Do you have today's report for this flight? Is there anything out of the ordinary I should know about?"

He shook his head. "No. One passenger had her ticket stolen. It was used so she is trying to get on the flight. It seems innocent as the woman has no criminal history and she works for one of your companies. I thought her story was suspicious until I retrieved the camera footage that shows the man purposely targeted her. I don't blame him. The female was an easy mark. She's poor, fat, and a complete pushover."

"What is her name? Which company does she work for?" I held out my hand for the report. I looked at Cosimo and nodded.

"While you give him the report, I want to see the video footage," said Cosimo.

"Her name is Ivy Johnson. She's a junior analyst at OL Investments. She has worked for you for the last four years. She came with her best friend who also works for you. Her name is Olivia Cruz. Ms. Cruz has been vetted. We are still doing a quick investigation on Ivy, although she won't be on your flight."

There was something about his tone that rubbed me raw. If Ivy was innocent, and she had been robbed, why was she being denied an opportunity to go to Hawaii with her best friend? Somehow, he thought it was all right because she was overweight and poor.

What a presumptuous prick.

"I didn't say Ms. Cruz was cleared. I give the final clearances therefore who cleared her?"

I watched him slowly swallow. "Mr. Salvatore, your brother. I had to call him to vet her since she works directly for him. She has been working directly with him for the past twelve years."

Cosimo rushed over to me. "I watched the video. The man who robbed Ivy was Aleksei Zakharov. I'm sure of his identity. It means there is a female hitman already on board. We can't rule out whether Ivy isn't working for them yet. If she isn't, I doubt they will let her live after this," said Cosimo.

I frowned. "How easy of a mark was she?"

He sighed. "It's not just that. She looks to be a

cross between a teacher and a Jehovah witness. Her innocence is the reason she'll die."

When was it ok to allow innocent people to die? If Ivy was innocent, she shouldn't have to die. I'd had enough of innocent blood spilled on my behalf.

"You have ten minutes to find the assassins. You should be looking for people who will be on this flight. Also, tell team two to be prepared to update me as soon as you find them. I want their names and their information sent to my phone before I return."

Nathaniel frowned. "Where are you going?"

I rolled my eyes. "I'm going to meet Ivy. Don't bother notifying the gate agent at the desk. If I need them to do something, I'll let them know."

Without another word, I left the office.

It didn't take long to access the other hallway and enter the airport near the HO ticket counter. I was prepared for many things, but the vision before me wasn't one of them. Her skin was the color of a rich toffee. She was five foot eleven, had hazel eyes and long coiled hair that fell in a sphere shape around her head. Her hazel eyes were striking. She had curves in all the right places. I would never call her fat. You know what they say. The darker the berry the sweeter the juice. I liked my juice the same shade as my soul. Black. She might be innocent but she had a body like a goddess. With a pang of regret, I turned my attention to Olivia. As beautiful as Ivy was, she had already accepted that she wouldn't be flying to Hawaii. It was impossible to miss when Ivy's attention moved from Olivia to me. The heat of her stare sent an electric pulse straight to my cock. I became instantly hard.

Despite my better judgement, I met her gaze. She had been appreciating my attributes. She blushed and averted her gaze. Her stare hadn't been one of a stone-cold killer or one of a vixen. Ivy was shy. In that moment, she sealed her fate.

I'll put her on the plane. If she tried anything, I'll snap her neck. If she doesn't, I'll wrap my hand around her throat and fuck her until she comes all over me.

Ivy cleared her throat. "Olivia, you're going to miss your flight."

Olivia seemed just as frustrated as Ivy.

Good.

Real friends didn't allow their friends to be door mats. I stepped in Olivia's path, and she ran into me. Instead of stepping back, I gently held her elbow.

She frowned at me. "This is America, and my blouse is Balenciaga. Release me now before I scream for security."

I was tempted to allow her to scream and show her that I owned security too. There was no one in the city who could fuck with me, except Luca, and his alliance.

"Marsha, give the woman the first-class seat."

Now that Ivy was getting on the plane and sitting

next to me, I would take care of her. My phone vibrated, and I moved to the side to answer it.

"Boss, the woman is Zhanna Egorova and the male is Makar Tarasov. I'm sure of the male, since that one time we attacked Ioakim right after Gisella...."

Cosimo's voice trailed off but I knew the time about which he was talking. It was the only time I lost my mind and went to wipe out Ioakim. I didn't plan or care whether I died. The grief of burying my wife and instantly becoming a single parent had numbed me. My phone vibrated, and all the information started downloading to my phone.

"Great work."

My left ear twitched as I heard Koloda talking to Ivy. Normally I didn't care that he was overly aggressive and never allowed anyone male or female close to me, but it irked me now. To him, Ivy wasn't any different than the millions of women who tried to approach me daily. Unless I gave him permission, he allowed no one access to me.

"Do you want me to brief team two, or fly out with you?"

"You take care of it personally."

After hanging up the phone, I turned to see Ivy and Olivia disappearing through the security checkpoint and running to the plane. It was better this way. For some reason, I was insanely attracted to her which wasn't good for her health. Unfortunately, she was already in danger. The Russians thought she had access to information they could get.

By the time we boarded the plane, we were delayed by fifteen minutes. It had taken a long time to locate Zhanna and draw her to me. As soon as I stepped away from my men inside the employee change area, she followed me.

Taking out my gun, I attached the silencer.

Once it was on, I hid behind the thick panel, where the flight attendants change. She crept inside and removed a hunting knife from a sheath. Opening the panel door, I fired two shots into the back of her skull. I texted Koloda to come hide the body.

It didn't take long to find my seat on the crowded plane. Ivy was sitting with her eyes closed. She was vulnerable and adorable.

I scooted by her, making sure my legs brushed against her.

---

*T*he weather was bad. It had only been a few hours but the flight felt like decades. The heavy wind, rain and thunderstorms made the flight horrible. The turbulence was heavy and constant. There were times I was certain we would plummet to our deaths. Ivy had a death grip on my hand. Her jagged nails had drawn blood. The weather had thrown a monkey wrench in my plans to get to know her. It was obvious that she was afraid of flying and this flight didn't help.

I took out my phone and texted the pilot, telling him to land at the nearest city. All the passengers were to be rebooked on the earliest through flight in the morning. A delightful hotel, hot food and soft jazz could really set the atmosphere. The pilot texted me back saying that he would land in Houston Texas. My lips curved since I owned a hotel a short distance from the airport. I booked Ivy a room and alerted the manager to have my penthouse suite prepared in twenty minutes. I was certain I could go over her short life history in an hour before picking her up for dinner. She was only twenty-one, which meant she had started working for my company out of high school.

Ivy thought she needed my strength to endure this hellish flight but that wasn't all she needed. She needed me to sate the lust I stirred in her blood, and she was going to get it.

CHAPTER 3

IVY

MANHATTAN, NEW YORK

I nodded, backed up, and looked at Olivia as we rushed toward the security gate. The likelihood that I would ever get a chance to say thank you and give the man my number was like catching lightning in a bottle. Pushing aside disappointment, I focused on getting through security and boarding the plane. With relief, I handed the guard my ticket.

After clearing security, I ran behind Olivia, who managed to find our gate with ease. The gate was empty and two agents were standing on either side of the door taking tickets to board the plane.

Breathlessly, I handed the female my ticket and followed Olivia down the walkway to the plane. The plane was packed and there weren't many empty seats. When we reached first class and Olivia found her window seat I sighed. I found my aisle seat which was empty. It was a seat next to an empty spacious window seat. After I glanced at my watch, I noticed we should have taken off by now, yet the plane door was still open. As I looked around, I saw that the plane was full. The only seat available was the one next to me.

A gentleman wearing a Rolex cleared his throat. "Why aren't we leaving? Weren't we supposed to leave fifteen minutes ago?"

The flight attendant plastered on a smile. "Yes. Well, we still have one person that hasn't boarded."

"Leave him. If he can afford a first-class ticket then he can afford to catch another flight or be on time," he said.

She nodded. "Yes, he can. However, he owns this airline, so we won't be leaving him."

I stifled a giggle.

Wait. That means he will be sitting next to me.

For a second, I allowed myself to dream that the passenger sitting next to me would be the handsome stranger. Life had given me lemons, now I was going to make lemonade. I tried to relax as my stomach clenched. A salty ocean breeze drifted to my nose and I inhaled deeper. The scent calmed me and the stress in my body eased. I opened my eyes as something brushed against me.

He smiled. "Sorry, I'm late."

I nodded. "I want to thank you for what you did."

The handsome stranger responsible for me being

able to fly today had just apologized for his tardiness. There were six more men dressed as security guards were also on the flight despite there were no more seats available.

"No need to worry," he said.

I was so deep in thought that I hardly felt the fear I had as the plane soared toward the sky. The last thing I wanted to do was show him that I was terrified of flying. Unlike most people who flew often, I preferred my feet firmly planted on the ground. It wasn't long before the turbulence became a constant factor for the flight. My nervousness was forgotten as a flash of lightning streaked across the sky. After a loud crack of thunder, the heavy rain started to fall.

He placed his hand on mine. "Ivy there's no reason to be afraid. If the storm becomes bad enough the plane will land. We value safety over anything else. "Don't worry," he said.

His warmth comforted me and I needed some of his strength. Slowly opening my eyes, I looked out the window and frowned at the sight, I couldn't see anything.

How is the pilot seeing?

Squeezing his hand, I stared at him. "Thanks, I don't like heights. This storm looks bad. I can't see anything out there."

As the plane rocked with several winds the seatbelt sign illuminated.

The intercom chimed then the pilot's voice spoke. "Due to heavy storms, we will land in Houston, Texas. Everyone on board will be put on flight 878 to Hawaii in the morning. After you deplane, stop at gate seven to pick up your ticket."

My heart fluttered in my chest and I wanted to vomit. I couldn't wait to get out of this storm. I was grateful that Olivia was here. I had never been to Texas and we could share a room. There was safety in numbers.

"Is this your first time flying?"

Shaking my head, I sighed. "No. I just prefer situations where I'm in control and my feet are on the ground."

His lips curved. "You're a control freak. We have that in common."

The way he stared at me had me struggling to breathe. His penetrating gaze heated me from the inside out. The plane started to descend and my anxiety eased. I knew that we would be on the ground shortly. It wasn't a holiday, so the likelihood that we could get a room at the last minute was high.

"Ivy, I happen to have a room here in Houston. If it isn't any trouble, I would like to help you get a hotel room for the night. Would you like to have dinner with me?"

Once again, he was solving my problems. Dinner with him sounded like heaven.

I searched his face. "I'm a little jealous that you know my name and I don't know yours."

"My name is Leonardo." His fingers traced tiny circles over my hand.

"Once Olivia and I get settled. I'd love to have dinner with you."

It hadn't taken long for Olivia to get our replacement tickets for the morning.

She handed me my ticket. "Here is your ticket. We need to try to get a room for the night."

After putting my ticket safely away in my purse, I smiled. "We have a room already. Leonardo has helped us get a room, and I'm going to dinner with him tonight."

Her eyes widened. "He's smoking hot. Remind me to give you some condoms before you go to dinner."

I rubbed my neck. "I agreed to dinner but nothing else. Be quiet, here he comes."

Leonardo stopped in front of me. "Do you see the tallest high rise building right there?"

Turning, I looked out the window and saw the building he talked about.

*It didn't appear to be far from the airp*ort.

"Yes, I see it."

"That's the hotel. I have a room for you two. Chef Pierre makes a wonderful steak. I have a limousine outside we can leave whenever you are ready."

Olivia's eyes narrowed. She took out her phone and

quickly snapped a picture of him. "I'm sure you understand. A woman can never be too safe. What is your name?"

He raised an eyebrow. Leonardo Ottaviano."

She frowned. "Maybe it's a coincidence, but my boss has the same last name."

He tilted his head. "What is your boss's name?"

"His name is Salvatore Ottaviano."

"He's, my brother."

Olivia's mouth opened wide.

I laughed. "Something tells me your brother's not seventy-five years old."

Leonardo shook his head. "No, he is younger than me."

Olivia glared.

Just then four men wearing dark suits and black gloves appeared at his side. They looked mean and none of them had laugh lines. His security made me nervous, but I suspected as a wealthy man, he had many threats.

He glanced up from his phone. "The car is out front. Shall we go?"

"Lead the way." Smiling, I followed him out of the airport.

Olivia was uncharacteristically quiet and I knew she was thinking about her boss. As we went outside the frigid wind whipped around me, and I shuddered. I stifled a scream when two men stepped from the shadows and walked behind us.

Leonardo looked at me. "Don't worry. You are safe."

The men took our luggage and arranged it in the trunk. When Olivia went to slide in the car next to him, a security guard stopped her. I slid inside next to him. He somehow looked more beautiful in the pale moonlight than he did under the dull lights in the airport.

His hand cupped my cheek, right before he leaned in and nibbled my ear. "If you keep looking at me like that, we won't make it to the hotel."

My face felt hot. I was going to dinner with the most handsome man I had ever seen. He was charismatic, and highly intelligent. It was unreal that a man who looked like that was interested in a curvy girl like me. There was no way I could eat in front of him. I would order a salad and eat again after I returned to the room.

What would a girl like me do with a man like him? Would he ask me up for a nightcap? What would I say?

I was never the type of woman who had random sex with people or engaged in one-night stands. I barely had sex with my boyfriend because it was never the mind-blowing experience, everyone made it out to be. Now, I wasn't emotionally ready to give anything to anyone. I didn't know what to do with this man. He had to be a sexual god.

It wasn't long before the car pulled up to the hotel entrance, and the driver opened the door to let Leonardo out. As I placed my hand in his, he gently pulled me out. He looked like he wanted to devour me. My heart raced as he bent and brushed his lips over mine. Leonardo led me inside the hotel like he owned it. As soon as the manager saw him, she handed him four rooms keys.

He turned to me. "Here is your room key. You two will be staying in room thirty-two. I'm staying in the penthouse on the top floor. I'd like to pick you up in an hour. Is that enough time for you to get settled?"

No. You're looking at me like you're going to eat me for dinner.

"That's fine. I'll see you then." Taking my carry on from his security guard, we strolled to the elevator.

Once the doors closed, I turned to Olivia. "I agreed to dinner but I'm regretting it. Did you see that look? He looked like he wanted to eat me."

She snorted. "That look was so hot even my panties are damp and he wasn't looking at me. Bitch, if you don't have sex with him, I'll never let you live it down."

Leaning my head against the elevator wall, I closed my eyes. Olivia, who was usually the voice of reason, wasn't helping me right now.

"We're going up to the room. I'm going to give you

the talk because you need to fuck him like it's the last time, you'll ever fuck anyone. He's a gentleman, nice, rich, and totally into you."

"You're not helping."

She rolled her eyes. "Don't let Antonio give you a complex. He's the one who cheated on you. He wasted your time, and made you believe he was the one. He was selfish, manipulative, and didn't deserve you. Now take this night to live a little."

Antonio was a douche bag. He deserved to have his dick fall off. I was grateful I never let him remove his condom like he wanted to.

"I want you to sit on Leonardo's face until he chokes." The doors opened, and I stared at her. "What? I doubt that's what he has in mind. A man like him doesn't go down on women."

"He would brave death for you girl. The look he gave you earlier said he's willing to do it."

"Olivia, I need you to talk me out of this. He's going to his room to change and I have nothing to wear."

"I have a new dress I bought from Neiman Marcus. It's too big for me but it will fit you perfectly." She dressed provocatively but I guess beggars couldn't be choosers. I'd be surprised if I could even get in the darn dress.

I slid the key in the reader and opened our room door.

After leaning my luggage against the wall, I stared at her. "Let me see the dress you're talking about."

Olivia squealed and tossed her bag on the bed. After she searched for over ten minutes, she took out the most beautiful dress I had ever seen. My eyes became large when I saw the price tag. It cost over five thousand dollars. I stared at her and shook my head. "There's no way that I can wear this. My body is too large and this is too expensive to borrow. This dang dress costs a mortgage payment."

"You will wear this. Tonight, you will be his obsession. Who knows what might happen after tonight," said Olivia.

I rolled my eyes. "He's going to fuck me and I'm going to wake up to an empty bed, or whatever is the usual protocol for one-night stands."

She shrugged. "You never know."

After the fastest shower ever, I got dressed. I used my new lotion that was in my purse. It had a light clean fragrance that was nice and unassuming. I was seated on the bed, with one of Olivia's clutch purses in my hand. It was so small it only held condoms, lip gloss, and a credit card. The strong knock on the door made me jump as Olivia rushed to answer it.

Leonardo walked inside. "Are you ready?"

"Yes." I placed my hand inside his and allowed him to lead me out of the room.

*D*inner was amazing. The thing that surpassed me was the flavorful food and his quick wit. Before long, we were the only people in the restaurant. The large space was bathed in amber candlelight. Although he hadn't allowed me to eat salad, he fed me. I really enjoyed the food selections. His long fingers feeding me made the experience intimate. There were several times when he stole a few quick kisses. I longed for a deep kiss. Once he escorted me into the elevator, he pressed the floor for the penthouse.

Oh my god. This is it. He hasn't even asked me to go to his place. Does he think I'm easy?

"Don't be nervous. I know you don't do this often. Unbelievably, neither do I."

At least he didn't think I was a hoe. My body desired him and I was going to act on it. This day had been exciting and it was because of him.

"There's something about you. I have enjoyed talking with you tonight." He moved a whisp of my hair out of my face.

Placing my hand over his, I stared at him. "I don't want this moment to end."

His lips curved. "I don't want lies between us. I want to show you why you are the most beautiful woman to me."

Frowning, I pulled away from him. "You said you don't want lies between us but you say that?"

"Your beauty is inside and out. I am besotted with you. You're a kind, honest person, and you put others before yourself. Who takes care of you?"

How could he see through me so clearly?

The elevator doors opened. He stepped out and turned to me. "Tonight, I want you to be selfish. Let me show you how a woman's supposed to be cherished. Let me take care of you tonight."

I walked out just before the doors closed. "I've never done anything like this before."

"Leave your burdens, frustrations, and disappointments out in the hall. When we have sex, you won't be capable of thinking at all." Leonardo opened his room door and went inside.

"I stepped inside of his room.

Before I could blink my dress was on the floor. He ripped my panties from me. My back hit the wall, and he lifted my legs over his shoulder, as he buried his face deep inside me. He was devouring me like a billion-dollar merger. Leonardo was destroying every barrier I had. My thighs clenched around his head and my nails dug into the wall. I screamed as the most powerful orgasm I ever had, wracked my body. Unlike most men who tend to stop when you orgasmed, he continued flicking his tongue deep inside me, prolonging the bliss.

Before I could scream again, another orgasm began to build deep in my core. Tears slid down my cheeks.

Suddenly, I flew and bounced twice on the bed.

Opening my eyes, I saw him ripping off his clothes. My arms shook as I lifted myself up. The sight of his naked body had my breath hitching in my throat.

"I have some condoms in my purse?"

He strode gloriously naked toward me and crawled on top of the bed. His large hand pumped his shaft twice and he went down on me again. My eyes closed as I surrendered to the rapture. I lost count of how many times I came, as my nails raked across his scalp.

After what seemed like the fifth orgasm, I felt his hard shaft inside me. I was so wet that our flesh slapped hard against each other. My nails dug into his shoulders as he bent and took my lips in a punishing kiss. Tasting my essence on his tongue, I sucked his tongue harder as his strokes became harder. He hit my g spot. It hurt because he was so large but it also felt good.

"Yes, don't stop."

I liked it when it hurt. I wanted everything he had to give. It wasn't long before I broke underneath him. I screamed and jerked. He growled and bucked inside me. A warm stream of liquid flooded me before he collapsed on top of me. Both of us were breathing heavily as we laid there spent.

A wicked grin crossed my face, as I flipped him over on his back. "My turn."

I trailed wet kisses down the length of his torso until I met the thin hairy patch just before his cock.

Oh, how magnificent was his cock? Shit, he hadn't put on a condom.

"Bending down, I took his cock in my mouth. I didn't care that it was coated with our juices. He went from flaccid to hard instantly. I went lower and took his balls in my mouth. I was going to please this man. Normally, I didn't enjoy sucking dick but he tasted sweet like brown sugar, and I didn't mind tasting him.

His rough hands fisted in my hair. "Hell yes. Take all of it."

Wrapping my hair around his hand, he began fucking my face. As his large member hit the back of my throat, my gag reflexes kicked in. Instead of slowing his pace he stared down at me forcing me to time my breath with his strokes. My hand had slipped between my thighs to stroke my swollen clit as he groaned in pleasure. He was close. His balls tightened, but before he came, he pulled out and yanked my hand out of my pussy. Leonardo thrust all the way to the hilt inside me and pulled back and thrust inside harder hitting my swollen clit. My legs trembled as he thrust again and sent both of us over the edge.

―――――――――

*T*he phone rang.

With one eye open, I rolled over to get the receiver. "Hello."

"Ivy, this is your wake-up call. It's six thirty a.m. Are you up?"

I jumped out of bed. "Yes. Thank you so much."

After hanging up, I looked at the crumpled sheets. A sense of disappointment and anger surged through me.

How could I be so stupid? The asshole didn't even use a condom. Now, I'll need to get retested for diseases. Why didn't I make sure he used one?

Leonardo was gone. He hadn't bothered to wake me up and kick me out of his room. At least he had ordered a wakeup call so that I wouldn't miss my flight. My body was sticky from traces of his semen. After donning my dress, I slipped on my shoes and looked around for the room key. In a few hours, I would need to be up, shower, and put last night behind me. I walked over to the nightstand and paused when I saw the letter.

Ivy,

I didn't want to leave you like this but unfortunately something has come up. Thank you for allowing me to cherish you and catering to me as well. Despite my abrupt departure, please know that this is not goodbye. I will see you soon. I will

41

talk to you later in Hawaii. If you oversleep and miss your flight do not worry, I have reserved an extra seat for you on all flights going to Hawaii.

Until I see you again, be well beautiful.

L.O.

CHAPTER 4

LEONARDO

HOUSTON, TEXAS

I turned my head and looked at her. She thought I had a one nightstand with many women, but she would be mistaken. I hadn't touched a woman since Giselle's death. There was a benefit to being a Don. I never had much time for myself. My life was a series of seconds colliding into chaotic minutes. It wasn't until tonight, that I realized I missed having regular conversations that had nothing to do with life and death.

Why would I? I lived to take care of the family and my son.

My son's personality changed as soon as we buried Giselle. At first, I didn't notice that he worked hard to become an asshole. I had failed my wife but there was no way I would fail my son. It was my fault that his mother was dead. When I married her, I had done everything in my power to change my life, and I never broke my promise to her.

The soft snort that came from her made me smile. Ivy sounded like a sputtering train. Also, I found it adorable that a trickle of drool slid down her cheek. Her innocence reminded me of Giselle, except Ivy was younger. From the information I had on her, she was twenty-three years old, the same age as my wayward son. Hell, I was seventeen years older than her which was the reason I should've resisted the animalistic passion she erupted in me.

Why had I fucked her raw? I don't do casual sex.

Tonight, I tossed seven years of celibacy out of the window. I thought that my sexual needs died with my wife. Ivy's sexual inexperience and passion was a heady aphrodisiac I couldn't resist.

What do I look like? A saint. What if she wasn't on birth control? Why am I not upset at the thought that I had sex with her raw?

My cock twitched. Her tight pussy called to me. It was almost virginal. Viewing her recent physical was impressive. She had never been pregnant or had an STD. She didn't even have high cholesterol. Ivy was in great physical condition, despite her being over the body mass index for her height. Her curves were a blessing from above, and I knew just what to do with them. The tantalizing scent coming from her was making me hard again. I fisted the base of my shaft, as a bead of precum slid down my balls.

A green light lit up briefly on my phone before the room was shrouded in darkness again.

Grabbing it off the dresser, I needed a distraction. My eyes narrowed as I read the text.

> Cosimo. Isaak Korolev. He is the backup assassin now that Makar Tarasov had been retired. I'm in the mood for crawfish and gator.

> Leonardo. King Cake.

Isaak the rat bastard was in New Orleans. Soon, Ioakim would learn not to mess with what's mine. After I kill his men, I'll send him to hell behind them. Anyone who sought to harm my son, would be wiped from the face of the Earth along with their lineage.

I disentangled myself from Ivy's soft limbs. Within minutes, I was dressed in a dark sweat suit, baseball cap, and armed for war. I had more weapons in my throw away cars in the storage unit. After my other phone lit up with the address, I was ready to leave. A snore had me staring at the woman lying in my bed. She wouldn't take my absence lightly but it didn't matter. Ivy was mine. Walking over to the desk, I sat and drafted a note. Regardless of what I said, she wouldn't want to speak to me again after fucking her senseless and leaving.

I'll have to make her understand.

My life as Don was highly unpredictable, and dangerous. The darkness inside of me was mine; I wouldn't allow it to touch her.

After placing the letter on the desk, I quietly walked out. Instead of using the regular elevator, I slipped inside the hallway and took the hidden one. I walked out into the chilly night and got inside the car. My hotel lights began to fade in the rearview mirror as I pressed harder on the accelerator. My son deserved to live a normal life, outside of the mafia. His personality flaws weren't suited for this business. Giselle wanted him to marry, have kids, and live a quiet honest life. If it was the last thing I did, he was going to be able to live a normal life. He would never inherit the Ottaviano family business. His destiny was to dwell outside of the family with no chance of being sucked in. There was a reason his surname was Caruso like his mother's. After tonight, his acting out would cease. We were currently at war with the Bratva and soon the Cattaneo family might move on us as well.

---

*F*ive hours later, I was in New Orleans. By the time I hid my car several blocks away, I knew the layout of the small cottage where Isaak stayed. He was a paranoid bastard because he had a ten billion dollar hit on his head. A bounty I intended to collect. There was no doubt in my mind, the perimeter of his home was booby trapped. He was smart, but not smart enough to turn down a hit on my son.

The greedy bastard.

Unfortunately, his cottage had a hidden entrance accessible through the roof. I slipped through it without any problem. I crept through the attic and jumped down to the main level. The place was dusty, old, and had an overwhelming scent of mothballs. There was another scent and sound that I hadn't anticipated. A fat man with a Glock was sleeping in a chair in the den facing the front door.

Where had he found his idiot? More than likely, he offered the man a cash offer that he couldn't refuse. Now, he would die for his greed.

I took out my knife. My gun was equipped with infrared, but I wanted to catch Isaak off guard. This man would have to be a silent kill. Before the man woke up, I covered his mouth, and slit his throat. The one time I showed mercy had caused my wife to be murdered. When his body went limp, I wiped the blood off my knife and returned it to the sheath. Out of instinct, I moved to the kitchen and ducked behind the countertop.

Down the hall, I heard the bedroom door open and close.

Isaak was awake. I reached into my pocket and took

out the little device. My lips curved as I pressed the button.

Boom.

All the cars within a fifteen-block radius had blown up. Isaak thought he could escape but death was upon him. Aiming two guns at the wall, I fired several shots in various places to prevent him from escaping. Right about now, he would learn that the windows and air vents were also rigged with explosives to blow.

"That crazy bastard," said Isaak.

Yes, I am crazy, and my insanity has gotten worse without the light of my wife in my life.

Creeping down the hallway, I walked into the guest bedroom and ducked behind the dresser. Soon the bastard would come out of the room because he was cornered.

A door cracked open and Isaak ran inside the second master bedroom. He started spraying bullets everywhere with his AK. In no time, I was behind him. My gun was aimed at the back of his head. The air shifted around us, and his body tensed. He knew I was behind him.

He lowered his gun. "Why are you here? Why kill me now? You've had plenty of chances, what made you pay me a visit now?"

"You accepted the wrong job."

"Your son is your greatest weakness. His death would strengthen your position. You can't be everywhere all the time. Your wife's death taught you that lesson."

"Fuck you."

Bang. Bang. Bang. Bang. Bang.

I unloaded the clip in the back of his skull. When his body slumped to the floor, I took out my knife and severed his head from his body. After wrapping it in a pink blanket, I made my way back inside the attic. The police sirens were getting closer. I needed to be far from his carnage before they arrived.

Easy payday.

*W*hen my private jet touched down in Hawaii, my eyes felt like sandpaper. After killing Isaak, I was not in the mood to fly commercial with screaming kids and annoying passengers. I needed an outlet for my rage, before dealing with my son. I wanted to fight and fuck but neither outlet was available. Cosimo and my security team met me outside of my son's room.

"Cosimo, I need you to have ten thousand pink and yellow roses delivered to Ivy's room in two days. I want you to have an invitation drawn up for her to join me on the yacht on Friday. Deliver it to her room in an hour. It must be there before she arrives."

"Done, boss. While you were away, Antonio has

been a handful. He partied all night and had a three-some with some tourists. In addition, he keeps trying to ditch his security team which is why I have them in covert mode."

"Good job. After you deliver her letter, you can get some rest."

My son wasn't going to like his father and son talk. Hell, it might get bloody. I've always stayed my hand with him, but his recklessness had to end. I wouldn't kill him, but I might beat the shit out of him.

"I'm going to talk to him alone. Don't disturb me unless it's life and death." Without another word, I put the key into his bedroom door lock and went inside.

The aroma of sex, alcohol and ass filled the air. Whoever he had sex with needed to be bitch slapped on her lack of hygiene. His designer clothes littered the floor. There were several empty champagne bottles on the tables and two in the bed. Unlike the men in our family, he was passed out in the space between the bed and the air conditioner. If Isaak were standing here instead of me, he would already be dead. At this time, I would be getting various parts of his body delivered in an ominous package.

I snatched the champagne bottle off the bed and poured the rest of it over his face.

He jerked up. "What the fuck..."

Wham. I backhanded him across the face. "Get up.

50

These twenty-thousand-dollar bottles are coming out of your savings account."

"Why? You can afford a few bottles..."

Antonio stood, ripped the rest of his shirt off and wiped his wet face.

I nodded. "Yes, I can, but you can't. You dropped out of college and you were fired from your job. You always spout about how you are ready for responsibility, but all you want to do is spend money. There are prostitutes more responsible and financially savvy than you."

"It wouldn't be the case if you had given me an inheritance like mom wanted you to do."

"Giselle wanted you to go to college debt free. I sent you to five colleges and you failed out of all of them. In addition, you almost caught a charge for beating your pregnant girlfriend. You've already spent your inheritance."

He jerked the chair away from the table and sank down in it. "If this is another conversation about cutting me off save it. I already know you don't want to share your money with me."

"Here are the rules. You will not slip away from your security details. You will get a job and start acting like an adult. Doctor Messi will be here later to give you a physical and make sure you haven't caught any fatal sexually transmitted diseases. My enemies have no issues with sending you a diseased woman to snatch your life but that is the least of your worries. A billion-dollar hit has been placed on your head."

Crossing my arms over my chest, I watched him start to panic. *Good. This was his tough love speech. Issak was right, I can't be everywhere all the time. It was time that he took his security seriously.*

"What, a billion dollars. What did you do? You have money but you're not a billionaire."

Of course, I am. There are reasons you move in silence. There is no reason to show everything to everyone.

I shrugged. "The way you spend money, if you had an inheritance, it would be gone in two years. You need to decide if you want to move to Chicago, London, or Dubai. A change of scenery with new friends and opportunities would do you some good."

His eyes widened. "Have you finally relented and I'm heading up my own territory?" He grabbed his phone and started texting.

"Hell no. You would be dead in less than twenty-four hours.

The jobs are for program management. The starting salary is four hundred thousand, which is more than enough for you to start to get your life together." Frowning, I walked over to the table. My eyes narrowed as I saw the phone number he dialed repeatedly. Instead of leaving a message he hung up. "Are you listening to me? Who are you calling?"

Antonio rolled his eyes. "I'm your only child, your

heir and you keep me out of the family business. Despite making me carry mom's last name, I'm still your child. What will it take for you to teach me the business? When you die, I'm going to have no clue of how to run the family."

"It will never happen. Your mother made me promise that you would never be in the mafia, and you won't. This life was never meant to be yours. You'd better get it through your thick head that you will work, pay taxes, and live to grow old. Who are you calling while we're discussing your future."

"My ex- girlfriend. She caught me balls deep in Valentina and broke up with me. She shouldn't have gotten angry. I told her that I would marry her."

"You just had a three some. You are not ready to marry anyone or be in a relationship."

"I'm trying to get her back. She's just a fat nerd. No other man will touch her. She needs to understand that I need to have a variety of women, but I'll take care of her."

I snorted. "How? By giving her an STD. You can't take care of yourself. If she had common sense, she wouldn't take you back. Grow up and stop doing everything to get your dick wet."

Damn. Was Ivy his girlfriend? How did this idiot get a classy woman like her and fuck it up?

CHAPTER 5

IVY

PA'INA, HAWAII

*R*egardless of how I tried to clear my thoughts, I couldn't forget Leonardo. I was still a ball of emotions. When I crept inside of our hotel room, I was grateful that Olivia was still asleep. My heart was hurting and my body was sore. The last thing I wanted was for my best friend to see me covered in his semen. It was bad enough that I woke up alone. I wasn't certain what to make of the note. It was hard to believe that he wanted to see me again when he left me in his room. Without another thought, I walked to the bathroom, stripped, and stepped into the shower. It might be too late to salvage my pride in front of Leonardo but I didn't want to break down and cry in front of Olivia.

Unlike the day before, getting to the gate had been uneventful and peaceful. We were already sitting in the chairs in front of our gate waiting for the plane to arrive.

Olivia popped a strawberry gummy bear in her mouth. "Are you going to mope all day?"

I glared at her.

"Yes, damn it. I just couldn't wrap my head around what happened last night. Why write the letter when you hadn't bothered to wake me before you left? The letter is bogus. It was designed to make me believe he didn't fuck me and leave, although that is what he did."

"How can you discount the letter when he didn't have to leave one. You were asleep. He could've just left but he didn't. He knew you were exhausted. I didn't see you when you came in but the bags underneath your eyes show that he wore you out."

"We both know nice girls always finish last. Besides, I thought we had a connection ..."

Olivia patted my thigh. "I know men. He is into you. He meant what he said in the letter but I know you don't believe it. When he contacts you, I'm going to say that I told you so. Trust me, this isn't the last of him."

The weather was amazing when we landed in Hawaii. As soon as we retrieved our bags, we were met by Steve, who held a colorful sign alerting us that he was there to take us to the resort. We were picked up in a limousine.

I frowned. "Are we going to wait for everyone else?"

Steve shook his head. "You two were the only ones that were put on a through flight. Everyone else will arrive in five hours."

What the fuck? Did Leonardo do this before or after he left me alone in his bed?

Olivia shot me a glance. "I'm grateful that we don't have to wait five hours to enjoy Hawaii."

We walked inside the Pa'ina Island Resort. In less than ten minutes we had our room keys, a bottle of champagne, and a fruit basket along with a list of the various activities happening within the next hour.

When the room door closed, I threw myself on the bed closest to the window. "I'm starting to get excited."

She laughed. "Ivy, I've been excited for over two weeks. Let's get into our bikinis and lounge by the pool."

Great. It's time to show my cellulite and dimples.

I bought a high waist bikini against my better judgment, but the confidence to wear it hadn't come to me. A fleeting glance out the window showed most of the women wearing tiny bikinis on their athletic physique.

Lord, give me some grace.

It might get cold with all the drinks, so I'm going to wear my one-piece. I have a wrap that matches it."

"Hell no. Your sexy ass is going to wear that bikini. I would never let you look like a train wreck. I keep telling you, men like women in all shapes and sizes. Do you know how many women would pay a fortune to have your breast, thighs, and butt?"

What is the worst thing that can happen?

"Fine. I need to tame my curls with more curling cream and gel before I look like a poodle." Soon, I was dressed in the bikini and my hair was finally tamed. Turning, I made sure all my curves were covered as I tried to gain enough confidence to leave the room.

"Ivy, I think you need to see this."

"What is it?" I walked out of the bathroom. I froze as she was bent over reading a letter intently.

"This letter on the desk is addressed to you."

Why are you reading it?

A part of me was intrigued, but there was only one person who would have a letter delivered to our room. Although I had managed not to talk about him, my mind hadn't released him. I could still taste him on my tongue. On the flight, my mind had gone over every detail, as I relived our time together repeatedly.

"No. Let's go. There's a pool, a hot tub, and several swim up bars."

"He's invited us on his yacht on Friday. I told you that he was into you. You know what this means?"

Yes, I'm fucked.

Shaking my head, I glared at her. "No, I don't. I'm

already mad about how he handled our time in Texas. I'm not going on his yacht. You can go if you want."

Olivia narrowed her eyes. "You are going. You have deemed him a douche bag and the least you can do is get on his yacht to see if it is really an invitation. Then, if you're still upset give him a piece of your mind."

"Fine we can go." I said folding my arms across my chest.

"You must get a new bathing suit better than the one you have. You need to get the ultimate eye candy bathing suit."

I was already rubbing my temple to ward off an impending headache. Regardless of how I tried to tell myself not to think about him, he was on my mind.

---

*L*ounging at the infinity pool sipping pineapple flavored drinks made me relax and enjoy the day. I was no longer self-conscious about my bathing suit and I had even taken a nap underneath my tangerine-colored umbrella. The sun was out but the sunrays weren't as bright. It was still hot as hell and I was ready for the air conditioner and food.

I sat up. "I'm ready to get out of this heat and eat. Are you hungry?"

Olivia smiled. "Yes, all this alcohol on an empty

stomach has made me tingly inside. We should go shopping for a new bathing suit, and two new outfits for Friday. There's no telling what he has planned for you and I'm super excited."

Just like that, all the tension that left reappeared as I stiffly stood. "You shouldn't get so excited. I don't intend to hang out with him. Friday will be the last time I see him. I don't think I want to waste money on a man I don't intend to see again."

"Keep telling yourself that. Let's go." Olivia tossed her beach towel over her shoulder, and we headed back upstairs to get dressed.

Normally I wasn't excited to go to a mall, but the indoor-outdoor mall was massive. I was grateful I wore my comfortable shoes because I knew Olivia would go into every store and shop. After an amazing lunch, we began to shop. By the time we entered ten stores, she had twenty bags. I helped her carry half of them until I came across a shopping cart and paid thirty dollars to rent it.

"All your stuff has filled the cart. The next cart is on you."

She laughed. "I'm renting it now. You will not have any excuse not to buy things."

There were so many swimsuit shops, I rolled my eyes. The stores were ridiculously expensive and I really wanted to enjoy my vacation, without spending money on an outfit. Unlike the other eight shops, this boutique had designs for all body sizes, colors, and styles. A canary yellow swimsuit with matching sarong caught my eye.

After finding my size, I smiled. "I'm going to buy this. It's a bit riskier than what I normally wear but it's gorgeous. It will match my hazel eyes perfectly."

Three hours later, we were in line with our hands full. I had two bathing suits and two outfits for a night out on the town.

Olivia snatched my stuff and dumped it on the counter with hers. She held up her hand. "No, these purchases are on me. It's expensive in here and your date must be perfect."

I shook my head. "I can't let you do that. You've already loaned me your new dress. You will want to buy some antiques while you're here. Let me buy this stuff. "

"Trust me, you'll thank me later. Do you think he will invite some of his handsome, rich friends to keep me company?" She took out her credit card and handed it to the cashier.

"Probably. I can't imagine him having any ugly friends. We must stick together because we don't know them and we will be secluded."

Am I making a mistake by going? I can't let him charm his way past my defenses again.

Taking the stroller, I went to stand against the wall. Internally, I was panicking and needed to calm down. My walls were up again but I couldn't trust my judgment around him. I exhaled and closed my eyes. I stiffened as a firm hand cupped my ass.

My eyes flew open. "Get your hands off..."

All the fight went out of me as I stared at Antonio. I was relieved that a stranger wasn't groping me. However, his touch wasn't welcomed either.

I pushed him from me. "Don't touch me."

Instead of getting a clue, he sauntered over and pushed me against the wall. His body covered mine like he had a right to do it.

"You know that you're going to forgive me. We've been together for four years. You'd be an idiot to throw all of that away."

Trust was earned. Sadly, he had thrown it all away when he slept with his ex-girlfriend. I doubted that she was the only person he had slept with during our relationship. He always told lies and never wanted to tell me where he was going or when he'd return. There were many red flags but I trusted him.

I pushed against his chest. "I know all about the crap you've been doing behind my back."

Antonio snorted. "You will never find a better man than me. This is your last chance. You'd better get your mind right before I move on."

Slap. My palm hit him in the face with enough force to whip his head back. "It's over. I don't care what you do. You've been doing everyone since we've been together. Now, you don't have to cheat because you're single."

"Bitch, it's not over until I say it's over. I know that you're in love with me."

His lips came down over mine. They were forceful as he thrust his tongue into my mouth. I jerked away from him. After wiping his slobber from my face, I rushed out of the store. I was grateful that Olivia was walking toward me. She glared at Antonio. "Ivy, do you want me to call the police. I saw him force that nasty ass kiss on you."

"Let's just leave. I refuse to allow him to ruin our time here. He made his bed now he can lay in it."

It wasn't long before we were in another store far from Antonio. My anger had instantly faded and weariness had taken root in its place. While in every store, I saw a tall man, wearing a Kango hat and a black suit. We had gone to five stores for women, and he was, there. Each time he left and never bought anything.

Did Antonio have one of his friends following us? He was an asshat but he had never harmed me.

When Olivia came out of the dressing room, I rushed over to her and grabbed her arm. "That man over there has been following us. He's wearing a black suit and old gray Kango hat."

Olivia turned around but the man had slipped out of the store.

"Who's following us? I don't see anyone."

I know what I saw. We need to get out of here.

"It has gotten dark. We must get out of here and head back to the resort." I looked around but the man was gone. However, I doubted that he was far away. He hadn't wanted Olivia to see him. *Was he alone or did he have someone with him?*

"Ok, I've done enough shopping. I'll put these things back. We can get some dinner to take back to the room," said Olivia.

After rushing through the food court, we got some Chinese food, and went outside. The mall was more packed than it had been when we arrived earlier. Although I didn't see the man, I could feel his eyes watching us. My nerves were bad, and I had my small pocketknife in my palm. I was ready to stab anyone who posed a threat to us.

"Stop looking around. You're freaking me out. I bet Antonio hired someone to follow us. Don't worry, we'll be out of here soon."

The man looked like he was in his late forties, creepy, and dangerous despite wearing a suit. When we got outside it was still hot, but it was nighttime. There were several teenagers hanging out, laughing, and I was grateful for their presence. Too bad our Uber driver wasn't on time.

A limousine pulled up. I stepped back, then froze. The driver was the same one that had taken us to the hotel in Houston. He was Leonardo's driver. Despite the situation, every muscle in my body tensed as he walked toward us.

Is he here?

"Ladies, I am headed back to the resort. Do you two need a ride? It's a complimentary service for the OL Investment employees vacationing," he said.

Olivia smiled. "Yes, our Uber is late. Can you help us with our packages too?"

"Of course. Let me open the door and I'll secure your packages." He swiftly opened the doors and we slid inside.

While he packed their purchases in the trunk, I looked around, and saw the man who had been watching us.

He walked out of the mall, with a phone in his hand.

Taking my phone out, I snapped several pictures of him, some at close range. I didn't know who he was but I was going to find out. "There he is. Look at him good. I don't think Antonio knows him and he looks dangerous. At least I've got a photo of him."

Olivia gasped. She took out her phone and took a few pictures of him too. "He looks like a pervert. If we see him again, we'll call the police. I don't like the look on his face.

I was uneasy the rest of the way to the resort, we were safe now, but not for long. Every place on Earth was riddled with pockets of crime and this island was no different. We wouldn't be victims if we could be victors. This was Hawaii and the islands were expensive, so shopping in the mall shouldn't be anything out of the ordinary.

Why had he targeted us?

By the time the car pulled in front of the resort, I was uneasy and mentally drained.

"Both of you can go on up. I'll deliver your bags to your room," he said.

I took out a twenty-dollar bill. "Thank you so much. Let me at least give you a tip."

He shook his head. "I'm salaried. The company takes great care of me. Put that away before you get me fired."

"Thanks again." Swiveling on my heels, Olivia and I walked to the door.

As soon as I walked through the front door, I was grabbed and swung around with my back against the window.

"You and that hoe, just got out of that limo. "Is that why you broke up with me," demanded Antonio. His voice rose in pitch and everyone stopped having fun watching the spectacle.

"I broke up with you because you cheated. Who we ride with is none of your business. If you hadn't had us followed by some creep in a suit, we would still be shopping at the mall."

His lips curved. "Oh, sweetheart, I didn't have

anyone following you. It's the company you're keeping. Rich people have enemies and you do too. I'm warning you again, you belong to me. If any man tries to date you, he will get his ass kicked."

I jerked away from him. "No one is afraid of you. Leave me alone."

"I'm a beast at being bad. If this is how you want to play it, don't cry when you get hurt. Just remember, you were warned."

Antonio stormed through the front door.

CHAPTER 6

LEONARDO

PA'INA, HAWAII

Suddenly, Pietro's number flashed across my phone screen. My brother was in Saint Petersburg, Russia hidden deep in his compound. If there was anyone who could infiltrate a place it was him. He had the patience of a saint and was perfect at intelligence gathering. He wasn't shaken often, and he always kept a level head.

"What's happening?" I asked as I sat down on the bed.

A sense of apprehension flowed over me. I had a feeling I wasn't going to like what he said.

"Ioakim went crazy when he opened the blanket and saw Isaak's head. He shot two of his men then stormed out. I lost him for about four hours when he left the compound."

"He's at his mistress's house. I have men outside of there watching him."

His deep voice ceased and he shuffled his position. Wherever he was in Ioakim's mansion, he was hidden well. Anything could happen and I was ready for him to get out of there.

"You have the information, now get out of there. Don't worry about retaliation, I know that soon he will strike at us."

"Hold on. I'm getting an update."

The silence didn't bode well for me. War was always bloody and the last thing I needed was my brothers letting their guard down. We had a lot going on right now, and we had to stay prepared for everything.

"Damn. That asshole blew up six of our banks. I don't know which six but if I had to guess, he blew up our largest banks. That means we have a loss of about ten billion dollars. I'm going to kill him. It would be easy to slip inside his mistress's house and kill them both."

Shaking my head, I contained my anger. "Killing him won't be that easy. They are expecting us to try something. Trust me, they are prepared. I want you to go to New York and assess the damage. Those six banks were closed for upgrade. At least no innocents were killed.

I bit my tongue until blood flowed into my mouth.

The vein throbbed in my head, and walked over to my safe, and opened it. Taking a small prescription bottle out, I popped two blood pressure pills in my mouth. I didn't need to measure my blood pressure to know that I was at stroke level.

"We'll recuperate. Death is permanent but losing money isn't. We can make it back. You know how this goes. We came from nothing and like the Phoenix we'll rise again."

"Fine. I'll head there now."

"Don't lie to me. Don't do anything drastic or take any chances. "Brother, watch your back. Call me as soon as you've verified which banks, they were. Also, keep that piece of shit under surveillance. I have a feeling this is just the beginning."

My ears twitched. He was on the move. His steps were silent but I could pick up slight differences in his breathing. I remained silent, determined to wait until he spoke again. I was ready for Ioakim to leave Russia. That coward knew blowing up my money would send me into a frenzy, but I won't give him the satisfaction. Several minutes passed before I heard a car engine roar to life.

"When are we going to make our move?"

"When I stay the possible war with Luca Cattaneo and his alliance. We can't go to war with everyone at once."

I scrubbed a hand down my face. "I'm not going to

bury anyone else. Antonio has a fucking death wish. I can't worry about you too. Stick to the plan and trust me."

He snorted. "I trust you with my life. At some point, we need to escalate things. In the blink of an eye, he has set us back financially. We can't afford...."

"Pietro, do I look weak to you?"

"Never."

"I've been planning for these dark days. We took a hit but I was prepared for the worst. Don't worry, I'm smarter and wiser than that punk. We will discuss this later. Luca might take this moment to make a move now since we are weakened."

He sighed. "He could but he won't. Either way, I'll be careful."

I disconnected the phone. In a few hours, I would hold a meeting with my brothers to discuss our next move. After checking my gun chambers, I stalked out of my room. Now more than ever I had to see my son. I had no doubt there would be more attempts on his life. Reaching a short hallway, I stepped inside the secret elevator and went to the sixth floor.

Sliding my key into the lock, the door opened with a soft click.

Once inside I held my breath as an odor of sex, alcohol and feet filled my nostrils. I surveyed the room. There were six naked women in the bed with him. Something inside me snapped.

After several deep breaths I walked over to the trash can. There were several used condoms inside.

At least he used protection.

I walked toward the bathroom and stopped. The chunky white powder on the table caught my eye. I would know it anywhere. His Black American Express card was covered in cocaine. It wasn't my supply. None of my men would supply him. My men knew that it would be a fatal mistake.

I opened the door.

Felix was on his phone. "Get in here."

"You were supposed to be watching my son last night."

He shifted.

My voice was low and dangerous. I dragged him over to the table. "What the fuck is this? You didn't give my son these drugs so don't bother lying. Who gave it to him?"

Bending, I bared my teeth in his face. "If he gets any more drugs, even weed, you're dead. I took out my blade and sliced off his pinky. A half scream erupted from his throat before he stuffed his fist in his mouth and began trying to stem the bleeding.

"You have one hour to find out who gave him the drugs. Take him to my playhouse."

He clumsily got to his feet and rushed out of the room closing the door silently behind them. I walked over to the bar, grabbed the ice bucket, and doused the women in water. "Get the hell out. If I see you around him again, you're dead."

Their faces paled. They rushed out of the room naked, not bothering to pick up their clothes. My son was still sleeping. Antonio appeared drugged, inebriated, and fully sated. I threw the covers off him and punched him in the face.

"What? Do you know who I am?"

Before he opened his eyes, I grabbed him and body slammed him from the bed. "You're a dumb son of a bitch. You've seen what happens to junkies and still you do drugs?" Antonio's eyes widened at the tone of my voice. He quickly put distance between us.

There will be no running from me. I'm trying to save your life.

I pointed to the table. "What makes you think this shit isn't laced? Who are you trusting with your life?"

"Dad, this was the first time I've done this."

Bullshit.

Wham. My fists connected with his jaw, my elbow with the base of his head and my knee with his chin as he slid to the floor. I rained blows all over his body. His ribs turned red. I hadn't heard any crack yet, so they weren't broken.

The door opened. My gun was aimed at the intruder.

Cosimo held up his hands. "Boss calm down. If

you keep this up, you might kill him." He grabbed a hold of my arms and pulled me off Antonio. "There's some of Giselle inside him, you need to dig deeper to find it."

That was it. I could no longer ignore the entitled prick was nothing like us. He was lazy, rude, manipulative, and arrogant, while managing to still be a coward.

I jerked out of Cosimo's hold. My gun was aimed at Antonio's head. "Before I let that coward murder you like he did your mother, I'll kill you myself. If I find out this wasn't your first-time doing drugs, you'll wish it were when I'm through with you."

His eyes were wide as he sat holding his hands in the air like he was being arrested. Deep in his subconscious, he knew he'd better not utter another lie because it might send me over the edge. Out of my peripheral, I saw Cosimo helping him up. Without another glance, I stalked out of the room.

Thirty minutes later, I was in the gym. It was equipped with everything: steam rooms, boxing section, hot tub, and an infinity pool. I stripped and jumped in the pool. One of the lounge chairs had my blue towel draped over my gun. However, the weapon wouldn't work without my biometrics. I lounged on the side of the pool next to the hidden cubby hole that held other various weapons. It was another means of escaping a life and death situation. Soft footsteps made my ears twitch. I turned to see Ivy attempting to creep back inside the gym.

"Don't leave. I want to talk to you."

Her eyes narrowed. "I don't want to talk."

"I left you a note explaining my abrupt departure. I didn't want to leave you because the sex was over. Did you get it?"

"Yes. However, waking up to a letter is unacceptable. I thought we had a connection."

My lips curved. I stood as the water dripped down my naked body. I prowled toward her. "Don't leave. If you run, I'll be forced to come for you. Let me put on my clothes."

She nodded. "It's indecent to stand there butt naked expecting me to take a conversation seriously."

Wrapping a towel around me, I donned my clothes. "Despite what you think of me, I'm trying hard not to fuck the shit out of you again. You look good enough to eat."

Her blush rushed over her face, ears, and neck. She snorted. "Well, you sure have a messed-up way of letting me know it. Next time say it with your mouth instead of a pen and paper."

She swallowed a hard lump in her throat. "I've never had a one-night stand but I know you don't sneak out of the bed."

My hand covered hers, as I grabbed her chin,

turning her to face me. "We didn't have a one-night stand. We had sex after a date."

Unable to help myself, I kissed the confusion from her. By the time I had deepened the kiss her tiny nails were digging into my scalp. I pulled back before I justified having sex with her on the table.

"I like you a lot. I don't sleep around and I'm not accustomed to having unprotected sex. My senses were overwhelmed and I wanted all of you, hell I still do."

A look of distrust flickered across her face.

"I don't want you to worry about that. When you come on my boat, I'll hand you a copy of my physical, which proves the only ailment I'm having is high blood pressure."

Ivy smiled. "I can provide my physical results too. I can access them on my patient portal. I recently left a toxic relationship with an ex-boyfriend who tore me down every chance he got to feel good about himself.

Another man's trash is another man's treasure.

Ring. My phone chimed, and I gave her an apologetic look before taking it from my pocket.

> Cosimo. Josh Peterson. He lives in the Bronx. Antonio flew him here for unlimited drugs. He's supplied him with cocaine, molly, and Percocet for the past four years. The doctor said he failed his physical. Antonio has chlamydia, high liver enzymes and high cholesterol.

77

Leonardo. Take Josh to my playhouse. I will take it from there.

Cosimo. I just received a text from Felix. He landed in New York when he found out that Antonio was on the run.

CHAPTER 7

IVY

PA'INA, HAWAII

I frowned as I looked at Olivia. She was more nervous than a virgin losing her virginity. She had changed clothes ten times and was still not satisfied with any of the new outfits she tried on. It was crazy because she looked amazing in everything she bought. She was the kind of girl that looked like she stepped out of a model photo shoot.

"Olivia, you can't be this nervous about meeting your boss now that you know he isn't in his seventies and he's a workaholic. Just smile at him, shake his hand and leave."

She tossed her hair over her shoulder. "You can help me do that when we meet him."

Shaking my head, I looked down at my tank top and yoga pants. "I'm not dressed to meet the CEO of our company. I look like I've been doing Kundalini yoga because I have. I'll be just a text away."

Taking my pajamas from my luggage, I walked to the bathroom.

"No, put on something else unless you want to meet him in your pajamas. Don't forget about that creep who was following us. It's not safe for me to meet my boss alone. I don't know what he looks like and wondering around the island alone is dangerous."

Damn, she has a point.

"I'll be quick. What time do you have to meet him?"

Olivia bit her lips. "I was supposed to be there ten minutes ago."

Five minutes later, I was still damp with my shorts and half shirt clinging to me. I wasn't sure how Olivia had managed to get me to come along to meet her boss. What did she think he was going to do to her? One thing was for certain, being over an hour late wasn't professional or bound to make a positive impression. By the time we arrived at the fancy restaurant, it was evident the place had been closed to the public.

I glanced at my cell. My battery was drained. The hair on the back of my neck tingled, and I looked around. I couldn't shake the feeling that someone was watching us. She opened the restaurant door and shuffled inside. Without thinking, I took out my pocketknife and flipped the blade. The dim light made it hard to see if someone was sitting in the leather booths and at the circular tables.

"I don't like this. Why is this place dark and empty?

We passed at least a hundred restaurants before coming here. Let's go. When we were parking, I could've sworn someone was watching us."

Her eyes widened. "Let's go. I'll figure out what to tell him when he calls me. I'm surprised he hasn't called already. I'm over an hour late. He has a thing about punctuality. Let's get out of here."

He might be late too." I pulled her toward the front door.

The fact that the restaurant was empty with the door unlocked didn't feel right.

Who leaves their restaurant door unlocked?

Unlike Olivia, I wore my tennis shoes. I was practically dragging her behind me.

Olivia tucked her phone in her purse.

Wham.

I flinched as an ear-piercing scream erupted, followed by several loud thuds. We ran toward the door. I skidded to a halt, as the door opened and four men walked inside. Olivia crashed into my back.

Turning, we ran to the tables in the back. Olivia was faster than me and had already rounded the corner. Kicking chairs down behind me, I stopped to as a huge man came out holding Olivia by her neck.

"Let her go." I ran toward him and tried to stab

him in the stomach. He grabbed my hand and squeezed it until my knife fell. When he released me, I cradled my hand and backed away. My fingers throbbed. I was certain if I tried anything again, he would break my fingers.

Where did my knife go?

"What are you doing here?" he asked. His eyes were on Olivia but he still had her by the throat. I was confused how he expected her to talk."

Tilting my head, I narrowed my eyes at him. "How is she supposed to answer you when you're choking her?"

"I'm talking to you. You're concerned about her neck, but the men behind you have plans for your neck. I suggest you answer me while you still can."

Before I could speak, one of the men snatched my purse from my shoulder, breaking the strap.

"You just broke my purse. We were meeting someone, but we got lost. Please let us go."

Olivia gasped. "We were supposed to meet my boss, but I'm sure this isn't the right place. Please release me and let us go."

"Who is your boss?" he asked.

One of the men, cleared his throat. "Both of you were running out of here when we came in."

I glared at them. "Her boss gave us directions to this place but when we got here it was dark, empty and secluded."

"Fine, I'll tell you the truth, even though I haven't lied. Olivia, the woman whose neck you have in your death grip, was told to come here to meet her boss. We were over an hour late." When we

arrived, the lights were dim, the place looked deserted and screamed danger.

His eyebrow rose.

"We decided to leave. Not to mention, that a dangerous looking man has been following us. This place seemed like the perfect place for something horrific to happen to us."

He smirked. "Why are you here if she is here to meet her boss, he isn't your boss."

I rolled my eyes. "She's my best friend. Could you please release her, so that she can explain it because I can't."

His eyes narrowed. "No."

"Ok. Every since she was told she had to finally meet her mean boss she has been distraught. I mean, how hard is it to have a two-minute meeting with a man you'll never see again."

The men standing behind me started laughing.

"How do you know I'm not her boss?"

Besides your hand around her neck?

Placing my hand on my hips, I glared at him. "We've never met him," said Olivia. I've heard his voice so I know that you are not him. Also, he wouldn't handle me like you did."

One man cleared his throat. "I still don't understand why you're here."

"Who's her boss?"

"Leonardo told me it was his brother Salvatore."

His eyes widened slightly and his grip loosened a bit but Olivia was still dangling in the air like a rag doll. "How do you know Leonardo?"

I shrugged. "We met him on a flight."

"No there's more," he said.

Shaking my head, I looked at Olivia, but she was silent. *Why had the conversation turned in this direction?*

"I'm waiting."

I stared at him. "We stayed in a hotel in Houston."

His lips curved. "You stayed in a hotel with him?"

"That didn't come out right? He helped us get a room after our flight made an emergency stop. It was a beautiful high-rise near the airport. He had a penthouse on the top floor."

His eyebrow lifted. "How do you know he had a penthouse?"

I shrugged. "I don't remember, I think he told us. Can we leave?"

"No." He sat Olivia on the floor but his hand was still wrapped around her neck.

When I didn't see any way out of answering, I glared at him. "He took me to dinner."

A fleeting glance at Olivia showed she was alive. If

her chest wasn't rising and falling, I would've thought she was dead. Never in all the years I had known her had she been so quiet.

"You must be Ivy."

My face felt hot.

How does he know my name? Why would Leonardo discuss me with him.

"Who are you people?" I take that back.

My patience was short. I was ready to go. This interrogation was ending because I wasn't answering another question. "Never mind. I don't want to know."

"Fiorenzo, call Salvatore and confirm their story."

I rolled my eyes. "No, call Leonardo. He can confirm what he told us."

The entire situation was insane. All of this because we went to a restaurant. These men who looked unsavory were treating us like criminals.

"Sal, we're here at the spot. Caio caught a female named Olivia, who claims that she was supposed.... Uhm, she's unharmed but his hand is around her neck. She wasn't alone, there was another woman, called Ivy. Wait. There's no need to put Leonardo on ... Yes, I understand."

I watched as a myriad of emotions crossed his face. Most of them were hard to decipher, but the fear and reverence in his voice was unmistakable.

"Olivia, Salvatore apologized. He had an emergency but he will meet you on the yacht tomorrow."

The man's green eyes pierced through me as if searching for my soul. "Leonardo says he can't wait to see you again. Caio, their story checked out."

Olivia looked terrified. She still hadn't said anything but she didn't resist. I grabbed her arm and pushed the men out of the way.

"Ivy, I haven't said that you two can leave. Describe this man that's been following you," said Caio.

I took out my phone. "I'll do one better, while we were in Leonardo's limo, I was able to take a few pictures of him. My phone is about to die, so look quickly."

I held up my phone, showing him the photos. Instead of him just looking, he snatched the phone and began sending all the photos of the guy to himself.

"If either of you see him again, get away from him immediately and call Leonardo or Salvatore." He handed back my phone.

Frowning, I studied him. "Do you know him?"

"No, but he looks dangerous. If someone is following you regardless of where you are, run. Your safety always comes first."

We were back inside our hotel room, and Olivia hadn't uttered a word. Her silence was deafening and I couldn't take it any longer. "Olivia, your silence is scaring me. What's going on in your head?"

She swallowed. "What happened tonight solidified some things that didn't add up about my boss. Those people were made men."

What is a made man?

CHAPTER 8

LEONARDO

PA'INA, HAWAII

I was going to kill him. Antonio had to be slow or stupid. That little shit had fled to New York unprotected. He was an idiot to think that he could run from me. This entire situation was unacceptable. I sat unable to deal with my frustration. Everything was going to hell today.

"If you care for his life, you keep him away from me. I'm done trying to save his ass. He has a death wish and he's going to get it." I cracked my knuckles.

Salvatore sighed. "Let's get him back alive first, then you can beat the shit out of him. I'm sure he has a good explanation. He knows there are hits on his head. I'm sure there must be something else going on."

I doubt it. He thinks he can lie his way out of all the whoring and drug abuse that I would uncover.

My phone vibrated in my pocket. A fleeting glance at the screen had me answering it immediately.

"Talk."

My heart sped up as I waited to hear what else happened.

Did an assassin already gun him down?

"Boss, you're not going to like this. I just received word from Pietro that Antonio was sighted at our bank on the west side. When Pietro went there, he was gone."

"Why didn't Pietro call me?"

"He couldn't reach you immediately, so he called me. He's worried Antonio is going to get himself killed."

Pietro could take care of himself, but he would take risks to save Antonio. Hell, all his uncles would, which was just another reason there was no way he was suited for the life of a mob boss.

"I'll call Pietro now. There's a lot going on and it would be easy to be distracted. Triple the security around Ivy and Olivia. If Salvatore and I aren't back tonight, you pick them up and secure them at the safe house until we arrive."

His quietness was unsettling. He wasn't the silent type. "Spit it out Cosimo."

"Antonio's already made threats in the Ottaviano name. He's promised to retaliate until their dead."

Ignoring the throbbing in my head, I sat up. The

turbulence no longer phasing me. "Just who did he say that to?"

"He threatened Luca Cattaneo. Pietro infiltrated the alliance. He said don't call him, he will call you once he knows more. He thinks Luca might have Antonio."

"Fuck. Stay by the phone. I'll be in touch."

I hung up the line. Leaning back, I closed my eyes. Things had just worsened. The plane shook like it was about to fall out of the sky. The turbulence was bad, and so was the news I just received. There was no way I could avoid going to war with Luca now. If he killed Antonio, which him or anyone in his alliance could easily do, I would be honor bound to avenge my son's death or appear weak.

If Luca doesn't kill him first, I will.

Salvatore sat up. "You look like you're about to have a stroke. What is it now?"

Scrubbing a hand down my face, I shook my head. "Antonio just accused Luca of being behind the bombings of our banks. He promised to retaliate."

"You've got to be kidding me. If I didn't know better, I would think he was trying to either impress you so that you'll let him run the business."

I would rather our legacy be wiped from the face of the earth than see it in his hands. I'm ashamed of the weakling he's become. I refuse to take ownership of his cowardness.

Raking my hand through my hair, I ignored the vein pulsating at my temple. "I never raised him to be like he that." He's a fucking junkie."

Salvatore sighed. "You're upset because he's messed up. You're not actually thinking of killing him, are you?"

"There's none of me inside of this kid. Giselle was smart, brave, and resourceful. She would never cower before any man and she was a woman. He is no longer my son. I'm going to disown him or put a bullet in his head. Damn, I might do both."

Ignoring the heavy turbulence, I jumped to my feet. I was livid and sitting down feeling my stomach drop into my big toe was not helping. The only positive aspect to this situation was that she wasn't alive to see the piece of shit she almost died birthing.

She is weeping bloody tears from heaven. The Lord knows that neither of us would ever join her there.

"We can fix this. You always find a way out of no way."

Despite having no balls, Antonio had done the unforgivable.

"No, Salvatore, we can't. We're going to end up going to war. We are strong but this is the worse time since we are already at war with Borisov Bratva. If we go to war with the Cattaneo family, the Irish, and Russians will join in too."

We're dead.

I sat down. "We can't fight them all. We need to be part of the alliance. Now they know how weak my son is, they'll view me as weak Don for raising him up as a coward. They will never allow us to be in the alliance now."

Salvatore snorted. "Leo, Luca is smarter than you're giving him credit for. He still will not want us in New York but he'll think before doing anything rash."

"I wouldn't be surprised if the bastard attempts to put a bullet in my head as soon as the wheels bounced off the tarmac."

Salvatore was an optimist when it came to me finding solutions to our problems. This problem didn't have a solution that would get us what we needed. Any enemy would strike now while his opponent was weak and distracted.

Who would show mercy to their enemy?

I thought I had time to figure out an angle, which would show what the Ottaviano family could bring to the table. It wasn't like they were going to automatically trust us, and we hadn't done any business with his Irish or Russian partners. I thought I might be able to get through to Viktor, the Russian Pakan of the Vinogradov family, but not now. What was worse, was he would know we were at war with Ioakim and he could help annihilate us. As the Don of the family, it was on me. If I had to die to make the family safe, I would. Death had never been something I feared.

It wasn't like being in the mafia was a recipe for longevity, usually it was the opposite. Most Dons were rich as fuck, lived too fast and died too early. I had been building the foundation for us that would catch the eye of the alliance but not as their enemies.

My death is not coming at the hands of an enemy but my own weak, spoiled, good for nothing son. It's ironic the one man you would die for is the man that has orchestrated your downfall.

I laughed. The irony of it was bitter and exact. There was only one way to solve this. I would force my brothers to follow plan b while I delt with this alone. By the time they figured out I had sacrificed myself, they would be safe.

"Leo, I don't like the look in your eyes. What's going through that head of yours?" Salvatore narrowed his eyes as he watched me.

"It's time for phase two, and you all are going to implement it. When we land, I'll give each of you your detailed plans and you will carry them out."

"Hell no. Do you think they're going to take you out? We're not going to run to safety while you go to war alone. Ride or die Leo. Blood in and blood out."

"Salvatore, I have a plan."

He turned away. "Don't bother lying to me. I can tell when you do it. Do you think any of us would turn tail to save our own asses? You've been around Antonio too long."

Salvatore was a ruthless bastard and as stubborn as a goat. He never disobeyed my orders but he was putting his foot down now. *How did he know I was lying?*

He needed to think of his own ass. I was confident that when I was dead and gone, he would make an amazing don. All my brothers were confident, intelligent, and capable of running our empire. Marcello was the baby, but he was mature for his age, since he spent a lot of time with his older brother Alessio.

He stood up and walked to the bar. "You'd better produce an alternate plan because we won't abandon you. If you don't find a way out of this, we will go to war with those who seek to destroy us. It's that simple."

The plane was still shaking like it was about to break. It was comical that when I longed for the cold embrace of eternal sleep, death had run from me. I had been just existing. Now that I have met Ivy, I have started to live again. The tide had changed. I would have to forfeit my life to keep them safe, and I would gladly do so repeatedly.

"I need you to promise me that no matter what happen, you'll look after Ivy Johnson."

"Hell no. You're going to get yourself killed, right now? I'm sure you're in love with her. What are we supposed to do with her?"

He sat there sipping his brandy.

I'm obsessed with her. I'm not foolish enough to love another. I know how that turns out.

"You would expect me to take care of Olivia or are you in denial? You're in love with your assistant?"

Salvatore smiled. "I'm not in denial about anything. I've stayed away from her physically but I can't get her out of my mind She's like an exotic drug and when I don't hear from, I can't function."

Frowning, I shook my head. How my brother could admit a weakness, even to me, was baffling. Love was an emotion that opened a chiasm of emotions which left you vulnerable.

He elbowed me. "Do you know what the difference is between you and me, I am not in denial about my addiction. I've given into my obsession and I'm going to take her."

His admission of love for Olivia came at the worse time. We were right in the middle of a war.

I rolled my eyes. "When it's your time to run the family, having a wife will be one of your major vulnerabilities. You've seen how our enemies strike out at your wife and children. Do you really want to put Olivia through that?"

Salvatore smiled. "I have no intentions of dying on her. You won't be dying either. You're a freaking genius, and your IQ is off the scale. You're surprised because your original plan has been changed. In the end, you're going to see us through this; you always do."

I'm not a god. I'm fallible just like you.

Closing my eyes, I decided to take a power nap. I always saw things different after a nap and when my brain was not at risk for a brain bleed.

"Frankly, I'm a little surprised that you're so willing to die when you've fallen in love for the first time. I've never seen that look on your face ever."

First time? What is he talking about? I loved Giselle.

"I haven't had a look on my face. I loved Giselle."

"Leo, you look different. You even move differently. You're happier, excited, and hopeful. I would hazard a guess that you've made love to her. I mean fucked her raw, face to face, and eating her pussy like a pomegranate with cuddling instead of kicking her out before the nut dried on your balls."

Wise ass.

"If you recall, you didn't immediately fall for Giselle. It wasn't until she told you she wouldn't allow you to push her away that you stopped being emotionally distant. Over time, you fell in love with Giselle. You were never like you are now."

I held up my hand. "Are you a head shrink now. This isn't the time to discuss our feelings."

"Ivy is the one. I'm dying to meet her. Any woman who can make you come alive after you've been dead

97

inside all these years, has my internal gratitude and unwavering loyalty."

Ignoring him, I laid back again and closed my eyes. Soon we would be back in New York.

Several minutes passed in silence and I was grateful for it. Unfortunately sleep eluded me as my brother's words echoed repeatedly in my mind.

"Don't worry, I'll always do for you and yours until my dying breath. You never have to ask this of me or any of us. We are family. Did your recent taste of pussy cloud your brain?"

"Shut the fuck up Salvatore."

My eyes flew open as the wheels bounced on the tarmac.

After packing two duffle bags with more aggressive weapons, and tossing one to him, I was ready to paint the streets of New York red. Once again, I tried to call Antonio's phone with my number blocked but it was going straight to voicemail. I didn't have proof, but I was certain that he was alive. I would feel it if he were dead.

I smiled. "I have a feeling, Ioakim will have assassins in the city to kill us. Let's send him some messages shall we."

I ran down the steps. "We're going to split up. You go to the bank on the west side and secure Antonio if he's there. The explosions might not have penetrated the panic rooms burrowed underground. Check them at each bank and salvage anything that you can."

He cracked his neck. "Done. If there's an assassin there, I'll kill him on sight."

I nodded. "I'm going head to Pratt Investments our new agency. I just remembered that it's Thursday, and Betsy will be there alone. I wouldn't put it past them to blow up that location next."

Salvatore lips thinned. "Which means we have a leak. There is a traitor among us."

"Exactly. None of this is coincidence. Someone wants us weak and annihilated. It takes money and power to make this happen. Our enemies have targeted both."

Deep down I know who it is.

CHAPTER 9

LEONARDO

MANHATTAN, NEW YORK

I drove through the city like a race car driver. Salvatore and I were driving new cars that were typically for the middle class. No one would expect either of us to be driving an electric Toyota. Most of the time we drove expensive cars, but this wasn't one of those times. We needed to blend in and become invisible. Only my brothers and I knew of these vehicles, so the traitor wouldn't have that information. I had at least four hundred and fifty billion dollars in Pratt Investments.

Lucky for us, I had the feeling that our enemies would hit our banks undergoing renovations. It was why the bulk of the money had been moved three months earlier. We lost a ton of money but not what we could have lost. There was no way the perpetrator would get away with blowing up my money. Traffic was hectic as always. I kept looking at the clock, frantically worrying that I wouldn't arrive on time. Betsy was there all alone and she was pregnant.

After I was certain Betsy was safe, I would secure the rest of our money. We were lucky I was a paranoid bastard because this location had two distinct types of panic rooms. My personal panic room descended deep underground and could withstand any bomb. The other panic room was built for my employees and not underground. It wouldn't withstand every bomb, but my employees couldn't know the true nature of the Ottaviano family. We were upstanding individuals and not associated with the mafia. We didn't deal with the usual business.

This was one time I hoped that my instincts were wrong. The last thing I needed was for Luca, to show up and try to kill me. Instead of going the normal way to the bank, I took the alleys, and went through a secret entrance, which opened to a secret garage. I was the only one that knew of its existence and I never used it, opting to use it as an emergency entrance and exit only. Once again, my paranoia had made things easier for me. After the garage door shut, several low lights came on. I shut off the engine, rushed to the secret panel, and activated additional security cameras inside and outside as well as the bomb detectors.

Good. So far, no surprises.

Pressing my hand to the secret panel, I went inside.

I scrutinized all the security footage. Betsy was on her usual smoke break. The bank was empty and locked while she was outside smoking. I ran down the hallway and began moving the money. The gold bars couldn't be moved to the safe in case Betsy found the hidden money and secret tunnels in the panic room. I sighed and began moving all the gold into the safe. The safe was bomb proof as well but it was not underground, which meant it might not survive some types of explosions.

I monitored the security feed while I secured everything. A fleeting glance at the clock showed Betsy was late coming back from her smoke break. I was going to talk to her again about that. Her tardiness didn't bother me, but her smoking while expecting did. What I saw on the monitor made me freeze.

What?

The striking woman, with a face I knew all too well walked inside the bank five minutes after Betsy sat down. I stared in confusion as I watched Jasmin Maghrebi saunter toward Betsy.

Why was Luca's pregnant wife in my bank?

I was certain she wasn't coming to kill us and Luca would never have allowed her here. He would know that I owned this bank, and he would never allow her to do business with me directly or indirectly. Luca hadn't shared that little tidbit with his wife.

Pacing I thought about how I could turn this

nightmare into an advantage. My eyes caught a glimpse of a red car on the security feed outside. I quickly zoomed in on the male donning leather gloves. He was a Russian assassin.

I have a fucking assassin about to blow up my bank with two pregnant women inside, and one of them happen to be Luca's wife.

Without thinking I opened the safe again. There was no way I would allow two innocent women to be killed. I grabbed one of the small duffel bags with two hundred thousand dollars. I tossed in several secret trackers hidden in the inside fabric of the bag. Smiling, I also tossed a small device that was a remote-controlled explosive. After five minutes the device would emit a faint dye on the money that could only be seen under special lighting. A symbol of a fox would be transferred to anyone's hand that handled it. I was the only one who could remove the dye with a special compound I created. Using my personal code, I relocked the outer door for fifteen minutes instead of the usual ten.

I took the secret elevator to the main floor so that I could get to Betsy before Jasmin. Betsy would have to face the assassin, not Jasmin. I would put her in the panic room. When Betsy left the counter, she would seal them both inside. She wouldn't be happy if she had to face danger. What I wouldn't tell her is that if things went wrong, I'd kill this motherfucker right in front of her. I would have to violate my rule number one, no witnesses. Betsy wasn't just a great employee; she was like family.

Smiling, I cleared my throat. "Betsy, I need you to listen carefully. Unfortunately, we're about to be robbed."

Her eyes flew wide. "What kind of nut job is trying to rob us. Did you call the police?"

Hell no.

"You're going to give him the money that you have in your register, which I hazard a guess is not that much. You're also going to put everything in this duffel bag which has more money. Then, you're going to hand it to him."

Frowning she shook her head. "You want me to give him the money? Why?"

"If you don't give him a substantial amount of money, he will harm you, or ..."

Her face had gone pale. My words died in my throat as I thought of a better way to explain the situation quickly without her freaking out. "He's just a robber. Once he has the money he will want to leave as soon as possible. As soon as he turns his back, you run to my office and seal both of you into the panic room."

Tilting her head, she frowned. "Both of us?"

"A pregnant customer is on her way here. You'll tell her she needs to feel out some forms and lead her around the corner. I will do the rest."

I handed her the duffel bag. She hesitated to take it but finally took it a few minutes later.

My ears twitched as I heard the clicking of Jasmin's heels on the tile floor.

Hugging Betsy, I smiled. "Remain calm. I'll be with you hiding in the shadows."

By the time, Jasmin waddled her way to Betsy's counter, I was nearby in the shadows watching the scene before me while monitoring the asshole who was waiting out front in his car. He was attempting to shield his face from the nearby cameras but I had his identity on all my cameras.

"Hello, welcome to Pratt Investments. How can I help you?" Betsy smiled and stood long enough to show her pregnant belly.

"I'm here to open an investment account for my baby. I'd like to get a start on saving for his future college fund."

Luca is having a boy.

"Sure, I can help you open an account. I'm here alone, Thursdays are our slowest days. I just need to get the forms. Unfortunately, I can't leave you alone, you will have to come with me. The forms are right around the corner."

Jasmin looked around but eventually nodded. "Ok. My feet are killing me."

They walked around the corner. Everything was

going as planned until her eyes widened. "I'm feeling tired, I'll come back another time."

Before she could run or call Luca, I placed my hand over her mouth. I applied enough pressure to render her unconscious.

"Good job Betsy. Go sit down. You don't have long before the man walks inside."

I scooped up Jasmin and rushed to my office. After putting her in the panic room, I handcuffed her to the lamp that was bolted down. After she awakes, she wouldn't be able to leave the panic room or make any calls. After a quick search I slid her phone into my pocket.

Running back to the front, I was in position. There was no doubt that he would ask Betsy for some personal information.

He looked like a model. I was certain his looks caught his victims of guard.

He leaned over the counter. "This is a robbery. One false move and you're dead. Put all your money in a bag."

Fortunately, Betsy was afraid but efficient. She threw the money in the bag slowly because she had to bend down.

I could tell that he was getting impatient.

She hadn't noticed that he stuck a device underneath the counter in front of her. When she handed over the duffle bag, she didn't move when he took it from her.

His eyes searched her face. "If you want to live, sit down, and don't move. Have you pushed the panic button?"

Betsy stared at him. "No, no, I haven't pushed a button. The owner wanted people to see the button. The red alarm is to the left.

He nodded. "Don't move even when I exit the front door. I'll still be able to see you."

Her eyes widened. "I won't move."

I hadn't caught the type of bomb it was but I guessed we had less than ten minutes before the coward activated it from the safety of his car.

When he turned on his heels and walked toward the door, Betsy sprang to her feet and darted around the corner.

Great job Betsy.

Once she was out of sight, I ran down the second hallway and used my panic code to open the secret elevator. When the doors closed, I glanced at my watch. Two minutes and fifty-three seconds had passed and I was still in the elevator. As soon as the doors opened, I ran down the hall and skidded inside my office, grabbing a security table. My heart was rammed inside my chest.

Betsy and Jasmine were safe. Panning the perimeter cameras toward the asshole's car, I watched him pull away from the bank. He was driving and texting. I braced myself for the explosion.

Boom.

The explosion threw me across the room. My head hit the back wall and my world faded to black.

---

*B*y the time I regained consciousness, two hours had passed. I struggled to my feet and found the security tablet underneath the couch. After verifying that the women were uninjured, I knew it was time to call Luca.

I took out Jasmin's phone. Luca had called and texted over one hundred times. He answered on the first ring.

"Baby where are you? Why haven't you answered my calls?"

"Luca don't worry. The assassin couldn't kill her like he attempted when he blew up the building. I know you don't trust me, but I just saved your wife and son. The only thing standing in the way of the Russian assassin is me. I'll call you back with an address."

"I don't trust you, Leonardo. If you touch one hair on her head, I'll kill Antonio. I still might."

I shrugged. "You'd be doing me a favor. There's no need to send me his body parts. Your regular way of proof of death is fine."

CHAPTER 10

LEONARDO

MANHATTAN, NEW YORK

*B*etsy was safe. Instead of her going home, I booked her into a hotel in New Jersey under an alias. She had enough cash to lay low for a while. I had instructed her not to come to work until I personally told her to.

It was amazing what a few hours could do. Comfortably set up in one of our safe houses, I looked at Gavino. I was pissed that he brought Zeno, Alessio, Franco and Marcello with him. As a middle child, I expected him to protect his younger brothers and stay away from this war.

"I can't believe you came with him. Gavino what were you thinking?"

We were all here except Pietro. I had no doubt that he was hiding among Luca's camps. If they found him, they would torture him to death. Nevertheless, he was a stubborn, determined man.

Caio smiled. "From what Salvatore said, you wanted us to abandon you while you fight alone for the family's honor. We're in this together always."

Looking up from the security feed, I glared at him. "We have more important things to focus on right now. We have a traitor among us. Someone told Ioakim about Pratt Investments. He sent an assassin there tonight and blew up our bank."

Jasmin licked her lips. I saw a man when I pulled up. I noticed him because when he saw me, he whistled before going back to texting on his phone."

I pulled up the security feed and froze it on the man that had placed the bomb. "Is this the man you saw?"

Handing her the tablet, I watched her carefully and she plaid the video watching the man place the bomb herself.

Her eyes widened. "That asshole knew I was pregnant and he still blew up the building. I'm sure he saw the cashier's pregnant belly too. What kind of monster kills kids?"

"A monster like Ioakim Borisov. Salvatore, do you have the location of that fucker?"

Salvatore smiled. "Yes. Also, there has been one report of our money has showing up in New Jersey. The bastard is hiding out in the city.

Good. I was ready to cut his balls off and shove them in his mouth.

Jasmin watched us intently and I smiled. She was quiet and intelligent. A blush suffused her face when her stomach growled aloud.

"Do not worry, I have given Luca the address. I'm sure he'll be here shortly."

I stood up. "You must be hungry. We can't have that son of yours starving. Do you think you can eat Cajun chicken pasta?"

She nodded. "Yes, I'm starving."

Everyone including his baby brother Marcello was at the table eating with Jasmin.

Jasmin took a bite and closed her eyes, softly moaning as she chewed. "Okay, which one of you cooked this amazing meal. You must be a chef."

Gavino laughed. "We can all cook, Leonardo made us learn saying it was an important life skill. Leonardo is the chef of the family. Although he would never say it, he went to culinary school. He wanted to be a chef."

Rolling my eyes, I glared at him. "Shut up and eat."

Thirty minutes passed before the security guards picked up Luca. Over a hundred men were stationed outside.

My voice rang out over the intercom. "Luca, there's no need for those weapons. We're here eating. Come on in."

Jasmin dropped her fork. "He is very protective of

me. He's liable to shoot you in the head before allowing you to explain what happened. You should let me handle this."

Please. I don't think bloodshed can be avoided.

I nodded. "Your husband is a stubborn man."

Caio positioned his body in front of me like a human shield. He was the biggest out of all of us. His muscular body was built like a bodyguard. His lower half was just as muscular as his upper body. He was addicted to working out and gaining muscle mass. His body showed it. I pushed him aside just as Luca walked in with part of his army.

Jasmin stood. "Baby, calm down. This man saved my life."

Before I knew what she was about to do, she ran and threw herself in his arms weeping.

Luca had one arm around his wife, and his gun aimed at me. We would either come to an agreement or we would all die.

"Do you think kidnapping my wife, will save you from me," spat Luca.

She pulled back. "I wasn't kidnapped. I went to Pratt Investments to start an account for our son. I wanted to have his college paid for and his security solidified. When I got there, I saw a man. He was checking me out. He placed the bomb inside the building knowing that we were pregnant."

Luca growled. "I'll kill him."

"No, you won't. My brothers and I are about to pay the fucker a visit. I'm just seeing who else is involved. Ioakim Borisov sent him. The assassin's name is Kazmir Kuzmin."

His eyes narrowed at me. "His life is mine. If you refuse to give me his location, I'll kill you," said Luca.

She tossed her hair over her shoulder. "Baby, you will not kill him. He put his life at risk to save Betsy and me. You will not touch him. Trust me, I want the assassin dead too, but killing Leonardo would be wrong. He is an ally not our enemy."

"She's right. Zakhar is in Russia. Leonardo has been fighting a common enemy, Ioakim must die. He isn't lying about that sick sadistic bastard blowing up his banks and killing his wife. What he doesn't know is who the traitor is," said Viktor.

Luca's men swiftly parted to allow Viktor and his men inside.

I stood. "Who is the traitor? Give him to me."

Viktor tilted his head. "You were right. An alliance with Ottaviano and us would benefit us all. However, if Luca doesn't agree you're out. We have time to decide that. Right now, there needs to be trust to move forward from here."

Salvatore raised an eyebrow. "What are you proposing?"

"Give us Kazim. When the traitor makes his move, we will provide the backup you need. Until then, you will back us up tonight as we kill this son of a bitch," said Viktor.

He glanced at Luca. "Will you be appeased once you snatch this coward's life from him?" asked Viktor.

*A*n hour later, Salvatore and Caio were at my side. Our four youngest brothers had gone with Gavino to another safe house to await our instructions. Pietro was still hidden among Luca's men. He wouldn't reveal himself until it was safe for him to do so. He wouldn't leave where he was until he was certain of the alliance loyalty to us. If he found out they intended to betray us, he would destroy them all.

It was quiet outside the quaint one-story house where Kazmir was hiding. Why he hadn't left New York only meant that he was working with the Traitor.

On Luca's signal we all went to our assigned locations, waiting for hm to give the word. As soon as he received his signal, he kicked down the back door. He shot the man that jumped up from the chair. He had been sleeping and now he was dead. With Salvatore and Caio at his side we left a bloody path of dead bodies in our wake.

When I reached the bedroom, I pushed aside

Luca's men. The sight of Luca beating the man to death was scary. He liked torturing men. When he grew bored with beating him, he removed his knife and began to carve Kazmir into pieces. By the time, Luca had killed him, I stepped up and put a small infrared light to his hand. The symbol of the fox showed on his skin. I searched and found my bag of my money.

I tossed it to Caio. "You know what to do with this."

Viktor nodded. "Mikhail has proof that the traitor plans to take you out tomorrow in Hawaii. This is exactly what we wanted. Once the traitor was dealt with, Ioakim would lose his advantage."

We gathered around listening to every detail. For the first time in forever, my revenge for Giselle's murder was close. Everything I had ever wanted was within my grasp.

Salvatore smiled. "Brother, God has given you a chance to right the wrongs dealt to you many years ago. Let us go and prepare for tomorrow. Nothing will stop you from getting justice for her."

———

*B*y the time we landed in Hawaii my eyes felt like sandpaper. Caio and Gavino had made sure everything was ready. If Viktor's information were correct, there would be another attempt on my life. This time Ivy would be with me. It seemed like the dilemma of getting Luca and the alliance to trust me worked. In a few hours, Ivy would either accept me or not. It didn't matter, I wasn't ever letting her go. We would work out our differences and come to love one another for who we were.

CHAPTER 11

IVY

PA'INA, HAWAII

I paced the luxurious bathroom that now felt like a coffin. My period was never late. I could bet my life on my period schedule it was so regular. Despite the knots in my stomach, I stared at my phone. Just like everything, I needed structure in my life, so my period app on my device confirmed I was late. Raking a hand through my curls, I closed my eyes. Leonardo was old, what was the likelihood his sperm was still fertile. At least there was no way it could be Antonio's; we hadn't had sex in over three months. I had been regular for three months after our last protected sexual encounter. Despite his complaining, I never let him touch me without a condom. How could I be pregnant after a one-night stand?

If I'm pregnant, what am I going to do? He isn't

even my boyfriend he'll feel like I trapped him. This is too much.

"Ivy, are you alright? You've been in there for over an hour and I don't hear the shower."

Closing my eyes, I snatched a wad of toilet paper and covered the positive pregnancy test with it in the trash basket. Olivia would never search the trash can. There was no way anyone would find it. Everyone was scheduled to leave on Sunday.

After putting some drops in my eyes to clear the redness, I walked out.

Frowning, I studied her. Olivia was still lounging in her yoga pants and tank top. She had bought several new outfits to wear today and she still hadn't bothered to get dressed. I had a feeling she was trying to bail on me. She hadn't been the same since that night at the restaurant.

Oh no you don't.

"Olivia, you still haven't told me what a made man is? You know it's time to go to meet them on the yacht. Are you going to tell me now or do I have to ask them?"

I didn't think my threat would cause her to go paler but she was white a ghost.

She sucked in a breath. "It means a man is in the mafia. One of them is the Don, which means he is the head of the family and his words are absolute. It doesn't matter who runs the family, mobsters are lying, murderous, criminals.

Frowning I shook my head. "Where are you getting all of this?" Placing my make up bag on the counter, I took out my lip gloss and small perfume and tossed them in my clutch purse.

"For one, Leonardo isn't just rich he's a billionaire just like his brother Salvatore."

I held up my hand. "You made me go shopping and agree to go on this date and now you want to hide in our room. You were the one that said give him a chance. Leonardo or your boss are nothing like those men the other night."

Olivia sat on the edge of the bed. "You and I are way in over our head. When I get back to the office on Monday, the first thing I'm going to do is look for another job. My job pays me well but I can't continue to work for a man that is part of the mafia. What if I anger him and he takes care of me?"

Rolling my eyes, I laughed. "You've been working for him all these years, I'm sure you've pissed him off plenty of times, and he hasn't hurt you yet."

"Olivia, ever since you came here, you've been hell bent on not meeting your boss. Yes, they're Italian and there could be a possibility they're mafia, but their wealth isn't a determining factor for assuming that they are criminals."

Grabbing my clutch, I stared at her. "If we get proof that they are gangsters or whatever we will never see them again. You've already decided to quit your job, so just come on the date and if we see proof that they are criminals we will leave and take the first plane back to New York."

"I know you think I'm crazy but I know what I'm talking about. I don't think we should get any deeper than we already are with them."

I snorted. "The man was balls deep inside me raw. He came over my face and every inch of me and I still hungered for more. I hear your concerns but I don't think Leonardo is a murderer or a criminal. I like him a lot and I need to see this through. If I don't, I'll always wonder what it could have been."

Pulling her off the bed, I grabbed her room key and handed it to her. Every time we left the room, we both took our keys for safety. "Let's go unless you want to meet your boss in this room."

An hour and a half later we arrived at the dock. The weather was gorgeous and Olivia was still brooding. Her words had been playing over and over in my head. I had to admit, Olivia knew men better than I did.

It just seems so far-fetched to me. Am I blinded by my emotions?

My stomach was in knots. Olivia drove us to the dock. After we parked and walked down toward the boats her mood hadn't changed. I couldn't take her sullen attitude and fear a second longer.

I elbowed her. "I see how frightened you are. Let's just go. I'll leave a message for him after we check out and we're safely on the plane."

Olivia smiled. "Thank God, you've come to your senses."

We ran back up the path until four men stepped out in front of us. They were wearing dark blue suits, shades, and tiny little earpieces in their ears.

I smiled sweetly. "Excuse us." With Olivia's hand in mine, I tried to step aside but the men blocked all exits. The one in front who was muscular shook his head.

"Miss Johnson. Mr. Ottaviano is waiting for you both. Let me escort you to the boat."

My cheeks hurt from forcing the smile to remain on my face. "We appreciate that but an emergency has come up. Can you tell him for me?"

"Unfortunately, you will have to tell him yourself," he said. Without warning he lifted me off the ground and tossed me over his shoulder like a bag of wheat.

"What the fuck? Put me down. I need a tampon; do you really expect me to tell him that or do you expect him to insert it as well." I pounded on his back but he acted as if he hadn't felt any of my punches. Olivia shook her head she was being carried away as well.

"I'm taking you to him personally." My neck was

getting a cramp at this angle. And my fighting wasn't getting me anywhere.

Leonardo and another man who favored him, sauntered up the deck to meet us. Salvatore was handsome in a rugged sort of way. No man on the face of this earth looked as edible as Leonardo. The sight of him wearing khaki shorts and a loose t shirt made me want to jump his bones.

That is how you got pregnant in the first place. It must be the test. I can't be expecting.

"I'm so glad you could make it. Ladies how are you," asked Leonardo.

I opened my mouth but the fucker behind me spoke first.

He cleared his throat. "They were leaving. She needs a tampon."

Something akin to a strangled squeak erupted from my throat before I cut it off. I could feel my face heating immediately and knew I was blushing. I was so embarrassed.

Turning around, I glared at him. "You're so rude. We are ladies. Don't talk under our clothes."

Wham. I slapped him.

Leonardo chuckled. "You just learned how to show a lady some respect. You're dismissed."

Olivia and I hurried behind the men.

"Not you ladies. I'm sure you two want to freshen up. There are plenty of supplies including tampons, maxi pads, shampoo, conditioner, and other products below.

My eyes narrowed at him. "Why do you do have feminine hygiene products on your yacht? You said you didn't have a girlfriend?"

His eyebrow lifted before his lips curved. "They belonged to my wife."

"You're what?" I stumbled back as if he had struck me. His words were like poison barbs aimed straight at my heart.

"Come Ivy. He isn't the man you thought he was." She tried to drag me off the boat.

Slowly following her, I needed his last look etched on my medulla for eternity.

"The products were my wives. I didn't lie to you. I'm a widow. I donated everything to charity except the items below.

Frowning I studied him. "You're young. How did your wife pass away?"

His smile fell from his face. "Youth doesn't always protect you in life. Sometime shit happens. I don't like to talk about my wife."

Olivia cleared her throat. "So, what you're saying is your wife was murdered. I read that her death was ruled a homicide. She blew up in your car. That bomb was meant to kill you, wasn't it?"

Fate was a cruel bitch. How could I be pregnant by a dangerous man that was obviously in the mafia or up to no good. If he wasn't he still had enemies that were trying to kill him.

I gasped. "Oh God."

Olivia's mouth opened. "What the fuck is he doing here?"

I froze as I came face to face with Antonio. The bastard had brought his ex-girlfriend with him. It was apparent by his smirk that he knew Olivia and I would be here.

Leonardo stepped in his path. "What the fuck are you doing here? You and your whore were not invited."

"Dad, are you still angry with me? I'm grown. You can't hold it over my head that I left the island to take care of the family business you so willingly neglected. I was only doing what needed to be done."

Dad. This can't be happening.

Leonardo growled. "Get the fuck off my boat before I toss you both overboard."

Salvatore grabbed Olivia's hand. "Let me fix you a drink."

Antonio didn't have the same last name as Leonardo. Had he adopted him?

Leonardo held out his hand. "Come Ivy, we should talk."

Holding up my hand, I covered my mouth. "I needed to use the lady's room. I rushed down the steps and I ran inside the bathroom. After locking myself inside. I swiftly splashed water over my face, and some tears leaked out as well. Leonardo was a mobster, who happened to be my ex's father. There was no way that we could have a relationship.

If I'm pregnant I will raise my child but I hope I'm not. The thought of single motherhood shook me to my core.

As soon as I opened the door, the smell of the ocean filled my nostrils, as I stepped into the water.

What? There shouldn't be water inside the boat.

Despite my fear, I turned the opposite way and headed down the hall but I got halfway there and stopped. The water was higher and accumulating quickly.

Turning, I jumped and rushed back up the stairs. "Leonardo something's wrong. There's water on the lower deck and it's rising.

His eyes narrowed. He looked at Salvatore. "Have a seat next to them. I'll go check it out."

Frowning I looked behind me. "Is Antonio still on board?"

"A helicopter picked them up on the lower-level deck earlier," said Leonard. He quickly rushed downstairs.

I look at Salvatore. "Can you please call the pilot and have him pick us up. Trust me, the water is high. We need to get off now."

Salvatore dialed the number and put the phone on

speak. Right after the first ring, the call was diverted to voicemail.

I didn't have a good feeling.

Antonio was a vicious son of a bitch. I wouldn't put it past him to deliberately not answer and keep the helicopter.

They are rich. Don't they have more than one helicopter?

Olivia rushed to my side. "Don't panic. Let me get the life jackets."

What good would that do us? We were in the middle of the fucking ocean with no signs of land.

My hand clutched my chest. "I can't swim. I'm terrified of water. There's no way I'm jumping into the ocean with sharks, whales and God knows what other animals. Please Salvatore tell me you have another helicopter."

His fingers were rapidly flying across his phone screen. "I'm working on it. Olivia is right. Put the life jackets on and don't worry."

CHAPTER 12

LEONARDO

PA'INA, HAWAII

I came back upstairs, and I could tell Ivy was afraid. "We needed to jump ship now. There's an island not that far from here."

Ivy backed up. "What? You go. I'll be right here waiting for rescue helicopter."

Shaking my head, I approached her. "The water is not high yet but soon it will be up here and the boat will start to sink quicker.

"You go to the island and get help. I'll be right here. I can't swim."

"No Ivy, we are all going to jump ship. I can swim for both of us. You trust me so keep trusting me when I say, I won't allow you to drown."

Salvatore studied Olivia. "Can you swim?"

"Like a fish? I haven't done long distance swimming but I have no choice. I'm not ready to be shark food or drowned. If we wait any longer, it will be dark trying to swim to land. I'd rather see what is near me in the ocean," said Olivia.

"Ivy, you can climb on my back," said Olivia.

"The distance to the island would challenge an Olympic swimmer and you said your swimming skills were rusty. Let Leo, take her, he is used to swimming long distances." Salvador took Olivia and they dove off the side of the boat.

Without another word I scooped up Ivy and put her on my back. "Put your arms around my neck and don't let go. Despite what you might think of me, I've never lie to you."

I walked to the edge of the boat.

"You didn't tell me about your connections. You knew that I had dated Antonio. How could you keep it a secret that he's your son?"

"I'm sure there are things you haven't told me Ivy. Sometimes things take time. People don't tell everything about them on a second or third date."

Her legs tightened around my waist. "I'm petrified. Can we just get this over with."

"Hold your breath."

Splash.

*a*fter what felt like an eternity I crawled upon the white sand and rolled Ivy off my back and flopped down. Muscle fatigue and exhaustion had me feeling weak. The sun was going down but it wasn't dark yet.

"Oh my god. I can't believe you swam that far with my fat ass on your back. I could kiss you right now."

I lifted an eyebrow. Before she could take it back, I jerked her to me taking her lips in a punishing kiss. There were a lot of things I wanted to do to her and my cock was stirring to life. Once I got her fed and settled, I would secure her before my enemies descended on the island. Despite wanting to hold her close, I had unfinished business that I needed to take care of.

Pulling away from her, I smiled. "I hope you eat Mahi Mahi, if not you will eat mine. I'm exceptional at cooking it. Come let's get out of these wet clothes and into something more comfortable. I want to have dinner ready before it gets dark. We're having dinner outside. I doubt you want insects crawling on you while you're eating."

She scrambled to her feet. "No, and I'm starving. Are you all ok? I can cook, you know. You did all the swimming."

It would be dark in two. I wanted her to be asleep and safe while I had to deal with the threat. She didn't need to know the monster that lurked deep inside me.

It wasn't long before she had showered and donned a pair of my sweatpants as she came back outside. The food was ready and I had just set the table. There was a bottle of champagne on ice with two flute glasses out. A fleeting glance at my watch told me we had another ninety minutes before the island would be pitch dark.

We ate in silence. I was attempting to figure out how to get her to go to bed this early while I could see today's events playing over her face. She was starting to doubt if we would be good together. There was no doubt that she knew I was in the mafia and Antonio's father. Both points were hard limits for her, and I could tell she was attempting to erect her walls, closing me out.

She pushed her empty plate and glass away from her. "Leonardo why do you look so distant? What are you thinking about?"

"I want to get you situated and in bed, while I make sure the island is safe."

Her eyes narrowed. "Is that some kind of fucking code word for people are coming after us."

For a second, I thought about lying. I didn't want any lies between us. "Yes. I want to make sure as we are safe."

She swallowed. "Are you in the mafia. Is Salvatore the don, or whatever it's called."

"No."

I could see the relief cross her face and I hated shattering it. "I am. It wasn't something I wanted for myself or my life. Our parents were gunned down and we barely made it out alive. I had to do something to ensure my brothers and I were not murdered next to our parents. One doesn't ask for this life; they are born into it."

"How could you just say that. People don't answer that do they?"

I stood and gathered our dishes. "I won't lie to you. Come, let us go inside. It will be dark soon. Let me get you some clothes for bed. When the animals start making noise, you'll want to be sleep."

Her eyes widened. "What kind of animals?"

I shrugged. "Nothing too dangerous unless you're scared of snakes."

I led her down to the hidden bedroom underneath the house. She entered like she expected a firing squad to put a bullet to her head. Ivy was weary and shook because I hadn't lied to her about being a Don.

"Now, that you're down here, you won't be able to come back up to the main cabin until I take you back up. You will not be in any danger down here."

Her arms crossed over her chest. "What if something happens to you. I could die down here."

"Besides Salvatore, I'm the only one that knows about this bedroom. There's everything you need down here, a bathroom, television, a refrigerator, and games. It's for your safety."

Locking her inside, and enacting biometric security protocol, I made my way up to the main house. I quickly changed to a black jogging suit and loaded up my weapons.

I stepped outside and saw Viktor's creepy ass.

Viktor cracked his neck muscles. "I've talked to the men on the island with Salvatore. Half of our forces there and half are here.

"I expect both places to be hit. They can't afford to leave my brother or me alive."

Viktor leaned against the tree. "We have air support as well. Are you ready?"

I nodded. "I was born ready."

He shook his head. "It's not every day a man has to kill his own son. If you can't, we will step in and do it for you.

My stomach twisted. I had already mourned the bastard. Two tears in a bucket. He left me no choice. He was doing business with Ioakim knowing that he had murdered his mother.

Only a man with no soul could turn his back on his own mother.

"Don't worry. I won't hesitate to kill him." Turning away, I stalked off.

After I searched the island, I decided to take position a heavily thick leave tree. I was going to pick off our enemies like a tick on the dick. Three hours later, sticks crunched nearby. My thermal infrared goggles showed the men rushing toward the cabin with weapons drawn.

Yes. Walk into my trap you cowards.

Lifting my gun, I began to take all headshots. I had a silencer on it my weapon, so the men began to run everywhere. They also started shoot everywhere in all directions. It wasn't long before it was all out war. Ducking, and protecting my head, I silently shifted position and continued to take them out.

Several rounds from a semi-automatic interrupted the silence. The dumb ass hadn't even bothered to use a silencer. He was spraying bullets everywhere, and one struck the base of the tree where I was. Aiming, I shot him in the back of the head. The men had split up but most of them were dead on the ground.

I climbed down.

A slight movement through the water as I saw a silhouette emerge wearing a waterproof skin suit carrying an AK-47. He was shorter and scrawny. I knew who it was. He turned and spoke to some of Ioakim's men before walking toward the cabin. Antonio was comfortable among the Russian's men.

Aiming for his head, I pulled the trigger.

The bullet hit him in the neck. I quickly shot the

other men, then walked up to my son. I flicked a lighter so he could see my face while he died. As he made gurgling noises, I unloaded the clip in his head.

Six hours later both islands were clear. Luca had already called in a cleaning crew and all the dead bodies and blood had been removed. In a few hours there would be some early fishers and tourist out on the water.

Viktor walked over to me. "Congratulations on falling in love."

My eyes narrowed. "What the fuck are you talking about?"

"I know you love her. I can tell when a man loves a woman. You don't have to worry about Ioakim. You have bigger problems."

Frowning I narrowed my eyes. "What bigger problems?"

His eyes darted behind me to the cabin. "You must convince her that she can handle your lifestyle that she can handle you. Things are deeper than you ever thought.

Shaking my head, I sighed. "If I don't kill Ioakim now, he'll try to kill Ivy and me. He must be stopped. I will avenge Giselle's death, if it's the last thing I do."

"I paid him a little visit. His head is in your office. Go spend time with your woman. It's not often that men like us are able to find a woman that love us for us. Trust me, don't fuck it up." Viktor made a signal with his hand, and his men, followed him as he walked over to the plane.

I snuck into the bed with Ivy.

Viktor was right. Now that the threat had been eliminated, I could talk with her about us. I closed my eyes and allowed sleep to take me. When I opened my eyes again, it was four in the afternoon. Ivy was gone. I scrambled out of bed.

Grabbing my cell phone, I dialed Cosimo. "Ivy is gone. Check the entire island. Has there been any assassins entering the island."

Cosmo cleared his throat. "She checked out early this morning. She will arrive in New York in thirty minutes. She and Olivia didn't use the tickets the company provided; they purchased tickets from another airline.

Damn. She ran. Is Viktor psychic?

OM y lips curved as I laid back in the leather chair. I had arrived early to open the doors of OL Investments. I usually never came here preferring to work my other business, but that had changed. John Waters, Ivy's old manager had more sexual harassment complaint than an alligator had teeth. It was the main reason he was fired, along with a company email I read where he had held Ivy back because she hadn't slept with him. I wanted to kill him, but I'd settle for firing him for now.

"Ms. Johnson, please report to your manager's office." I had the intercom summon her.

She rushed inside and froze. "What are you doing here?"

"Please close the door. I'm sure you've heard that Mr. Waters is no longer working here. Until his replacement is hired, you'll be working directly with me."

She nibbled her lip. "Why?"

"This is my company. Close the door, so that our meeting can get started."

Reaching in my pocket, I took out the pregnancy test. "Someone once told me that withholding something constituted a lie."

I placed it in her hand. "Would you like to explain why you lied to me? Don't bother lying. I've had the DNA tested. I know it's not Olivia's."

Ivy scurried to close the door. "I didn't say it was."

"When were you going to tell me?"

She looked away. "I didn't think it was a good idea. I want my child to be safe and grow up without worrying if he's going to see his parent's murder in front of him."

"That's not your choice, is it? It's not your child, it's our child. You've admitted to withholding the conception of my child from me then you leave me no other choice but to take you to court for full custody."

I watched her fall into the trap of thinking of me as a heartless bastard.

"You can't do that. Her hand went to her flat stomach. I've just gotten used to the idea of becoming a mother. I won't let you take him from me."

In four strides, I had reached her side. My hand cupped her face. "I'm willing for us to be a family."

Her body jerked and she stepped back attempting to put some distance between us. Ivy's face was flushed and her teeth nibbled her lower lip. Turning away she walked over to the window.

She nodded. "Many people nowadays co parent so we can do it too."

"I said we can be a family. You love me and I love you. We'll raise our child together." I came up behind her and wrapped my arms around her. Before she could protest, I placed a gentle kiss on her neck.

Ivy's body stiffened before she turned to face me. Her eyes misted. "You love me? I love you too but I'm afraid that your lifestyle will hurt us in the end."

I cupped her face. "No one can promise you tomorrow. They can only promise you here and now. I vow to love you always until I my last breath."

"Leonardo, how can I resist when you put it that way."

WANT MORE

I hope you enjoyed Ivy and Leonardo's story! If you were intrigued on what woman brought the might Viktor Vinogradov to his knees, then click here to read ***Vow of Hate***.
Click Here: **https://books2read.com/u/mB5QxM**

Forced to marry. Forbidden to love.

Mila

Follow orders. Do what's best for the family. These are the rules I live by as the daughter of a mafia kingpin. Still, I never believed my malicious father would go as far as to force me to marry his sworn enemy. When Viktor, the Pakhan of the Vinogradov family, comes to collect me the air is knocked from my lungs. We'd met before, on a night when we kept our identities secret and were tempted by the sizzling attraction between us. Set to become his wife, I fear for my life... and my heart.

Viktor

I thought there would be nothing sweeter than revenge

against the man who killed my parents. Until I made his daughter mine. Mila's innocence soothes my tattered soul, the passion within her beckoning me from my darkness. One way or another, I will make her mine... mind, body, and soul. Her father was willing to sacrifice her, like the mad man he is. I will see to it that she's standing beside me when we bring him to his knees.

AFTERWORD

Getting Steamy with the best man
I Still Hate You
Brother's Glory
Hot and Bothered
Ivy's Savage Lust
(Sand in) All the Wrong Places
Arlo's Pleasure
Enticing Entanglement
Mutual Fun

If you are interested in joining us in one of our shared
worlds, please email us at absharedworlds@
outlook.com.

Be the first to hear about new releases, exclusive offers, and giveaways. Click the link below to get a free copy of **Callum's Vow.**

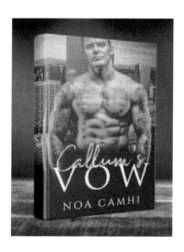

Sign up here. **https://noacamhi.gr8.com/**

Join Lashe Lacroix newsletter to receive a free copy of **Betrayed by Alcino.**

Sign up here. **https://dl.bookfunnel.com/xvx6dx3pqw**

Milton Keynes UK
Ingram Content Group UK Ltd.
UKHW020725290923
429627UK00015B/629